T0149362

MY
PEN
PAL IEN

Glynn Green

MY PEN PAL IEN

iUniverse books may be ordered through booksellers or by contacting:

iUniverse
1663 Liberty Drive
Bloomington, IN 47403
www.iuniverse.com
1-800-Authors (1-800-288-4677)

Because of the dynamic nature of the Internet, any web addresses or links contained in this book may have changed since publication and may no longer be valid. The views expressed in this work are solely those of the author and do not necessarily reflect the views of the publisher, and the publisher hereby disclaims any responsibility for them.

Any people depicted in stock imagery provided by Thinkstock are models, and such images are being used for illustrative purposes only. Certain stock imagery © Thinkstock.

ISBN: 978-1-5320-2008-7 (sc)
ISBN: 978-1-5320-2010-0 (hc)
ISBN: 978-1-5320-2009-4 (e)

Library of Congress Control Number: 2017908195

Print information available on the last page.

iUniverse rev. date: 06/26/2017

AWE Law

This document on a human's life is unauthorized for a human to ever read it. I, AWE, gave no permission for Ien or Cortez to share this document with a human. AWE Law and AWE Narration in this document is in unauthorized use but must be implemented because of supreme law. The punishment for the misuse of Ien's pen pal ability will be judged according to AWE Law. Ien will be subjected to punishment for writing a human's document at an unauthorized age. Ien will be subjected to punishment for sharing some of the human's original document with the human. Ien will be subjected to punishment for tampering with human documents. Ien will be subjected to punishment for sharing some of the human's tampered documents with the human. Ien will be subjected to punishment for communicating with a human. Ien will be subjected to punishment for communicating with a human when that human believed it was a possibility Ien was alien. Cortez will be subjected to punishment for communicating with a human. Cortez will be subjected to punishment for communicating with a human when that human believed it was a possibility Cortez was alien. Cortez will be subjected to punishment as the overseer of Ien, in which AWE Law was broken. This human document Ien sent to the human was lost by the human in 2005. AWE Law and AWE Narration appeared on this document in October 2009 when the document was found. You two humans who found this document in October 2009 should not try reading or exploiting this document for any reason but should burn this document to ashes. This document is not for the human eye or mind. Most importantly, Hysal Muke should never have a chance to read this document. You humans will break AWE Law if you ignore AWE Law. Going against AWE Law could potentially damage the authenticity of this human's document and also contaminate Earth life. It will also further alienate the human and alien race upon the uniting. The text of AWE Law and AWE Narration in this document is truth. I, AWE, have written.

lentro

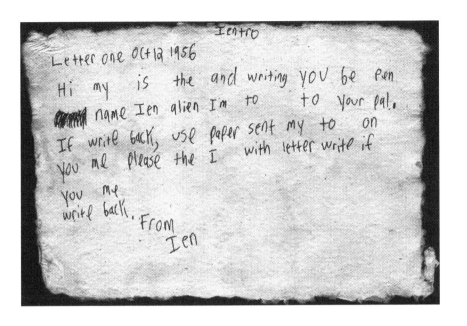

Letter 1, October 12, 1956

Hi my is the and writing to your pal. you me ___ please name ien alien I'm you be pen If write back, use the I with letter write_paper sent my to on you me if write back.

From

Ien

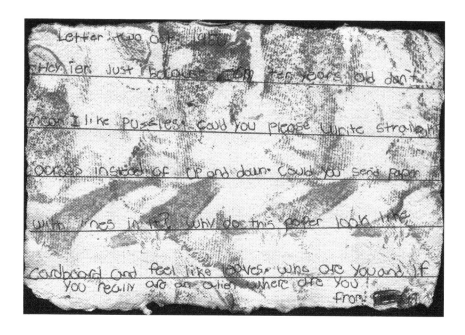

 Letter 2, October 24, 1956

Hey Ien just because I'm ten years old don't mean I like puzzles. Could you please write straight across instead of up and down. Could you send paper with lines in it? Why do this paper look like cardboard and feel like leaves? Who are you and if you really are an alien where are you?

From Donald

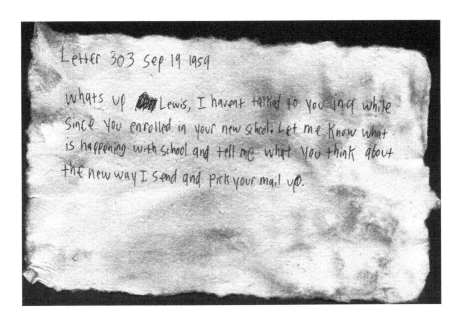

 Letter 303, September 19, 1959

What's up <u>Don</u> Lewis, I haven't talked to you in a while since you enrolled in your new school. Let me know what is happening with school and tell me what you think about the new way I send and pick your mail up.

Your pen pal, ien

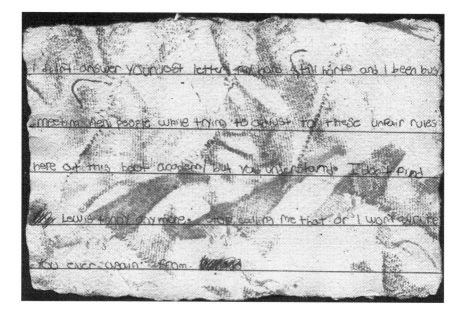

Letter 304 Sep 26 1989

How you doing my pen pal left, I must say it's a brilliant way you

do the mail thing from another planet. I will say it's more convenient

than the other way. I just still can't understand how you can get mail

to the earth but you can't get yourself back. You probably should pray

harder to your alien god. Also to let you to my planet. I'm sorry

I didn't answer your last letter my hand still hurts and I been busy

meeting new people while trying to adjust to these unfair rules

here at this boot academy but you understand. I don't find

Louis funny any more. Stop calling me that or I won't write

you ever again. From

8

Letter 304, September 26, 1959

How you doing my pen pal, ien. I must say it's a brilliant way you do the mail thing from another planet. I will say it's more convenient than the other way. I just still can't understand how you can get mail to the earth but you can't get yourself here. You probably should pray harder to your alien god Awe to get you to my planet. I'm sorry I didn't answer your last letter. My hand still hurts, and I've been busy meeting new people while trying to adjust to these unfair rules here at this boot academy, but you understand. I don't find <u>Don</u> Lewis funny anymore. Stop calling me that or I won't write you ever again.

From Donald

Letter 562 Feb 8 1964

Hi ████, this is my third letter without a response from you. It has been plenty of times you and I had arguments and was pen pals again, and I hope this will be another one of those incidents. I am sorry about making fun of your alien nightmares. I did not mean to say that you changed in a bad way after your promotion. It just seems that you become less tolerant towards our friendship and my feelings. If I can forgive you for mocking aliens for the creation of letters and words you humans use and

making hurtful embarrasing new words with my name in it such as MigratIen, I know you can forgive me. I also hope you are still not mad about there being aliens on your planet already. You do not have to be scared because they are not alsiahas, which are full blooded aliens like me. The aliens on the earth now are descendants of alsiahas that once lived on your planet. We are harmless just like the descendants and you will not even recognize them because they look like humans. If we the alsiahas ever come to your earth, our identity will also automatically conform to look like

10

humans because you are the most dominant specie. Einstein, Nostradamus and Tesla was some of the few humans from your planet who knew that they were descendents because their genius way of communicating with us on our planet. I hope you did not mean what you said about keeping me from your planet. It wont be like that Independence Day movie I told you about. I promise I will come in peace. I was just saying that people would think you were crazier for the reason of building the wall than the actual building of a wall over a planet. That was a good guess about the street

sign but you were wrong. Only the descendents on your earth will be able to see the message within the fiction book made to entertain you humans. I know you~~so~~ so dont keep beating youself up trying to find the message. for one, your not a descendant and due to the different forms of alien language you would be confused. Remember the book is the best chance for helping me and other aliens get to your earth. You will see that my mental ability to write your future life is a gift from AWE and not a lie. I will manipulate letters of words to show you the power of aliens. I'm not a fake psychic like you say. Aliens don't tell the future, we write it. Important events in your life will come from the words of my name Ien, alien, fen, and pal. I will give you a little taste of my pen pal ability. I'm going to write a man into your life who will be from the same state your from with a first name similar to the word alien. He will be a pro when it comes to predicting the next president. He will lick you as the

next president, but not the winner. I will write it where you go to a college with the word pen in it. A company with the word pen in it will be replaced by your first major real estate deal. Primary houses with the word pen in it will exist because of your hard work. You will visit a state with the word pen in it while running for president and there you will propose an act that will end illegal immigration of aliens. This act will be one of many you have planned for your first one hundred days in office if your elected. Speaking of one hundred. I made similarities between you and the republic nominae one hundred years before your presidency run. He is from New York like you. His mother shares the same name as your mother. A sister of yours will work in the high courts like one of his daughters. A sister of yours and a daughter of his will share the same name. I even made it where his vice president running mate and yours will both hold political positions in the same state. The first letter of your last name I will be used as bait. I will show you our pen pal relationship is not a accidental occurrence. I will replace the letter D and T in accidental with the letter P for the word pen pal. If that is

not enough pen work from me to prove that my gift is not a coincidence, I will take the letter of your first name from the word coincidence and replace it with the letter P. The word pen will help me choose the last name of your future running mate. I will write it where your vice president pick will be from the same state as the company that will publish my writing. That same state will have my name in it. A judge from that same state will also be written into your life. His middle name will have the letters P, A and L in them. I will also put the letter U in his middle name to represent University. The judge and your VP pick will attend the same university. The judge will also play a critical role in your univesity during your run for president. You will find it hilarious to harass the weak. I will turn the word hilarious to your political opponent. I will turn the word harass around just in case I decide to give you a women vice president pick. Her last name would also be made from the words of alien(Ien) and pal. It will be a president from another country who will also play an important role during your presidency run. Eureka is what you will shout out after discovering his first name. He will have my name scrambled in his first and last name. I hope all this evidence will be enough for you to believe

me. If not I will take the letter of your first name from the word evidence and replace it with the letter P, The word Pen will help me choose the middle name for that president from another country. I will also put the letter A at the end of his middle name to represent alien. Your God used Adams rib to create Eve and he brought her to him. Just like your creator, I will use letters and words to bring these people to you. All the names I give the people in connection with you will also be the same names I use to find a title for my book. Im sorry for not liking your song writing, but your bright future wont need those skills. please write me back

Hi, Donald, this is my third letter without a response from you. It has been plenty of times you and I had arguments and were pen pals again, and I hope this will be another one of those incidents. I am sorry about making fun of your alien nightmares. I did not mean to say that you changed in a bad way after your promotion. It just seems that you became less tolerant toward our friendship and my feelings. If I can forgive you for mocking aliens for the creation of letters and words you humans use and for making hurtful, embarrassing new words with my name in it such as migratlen, I know you can forgive me. I also hope you are still not mad about there being aliens on your planet already. You do not have to be scared because they are not alsiahas, which are full-blooded aliens like me. The aliens on the earth now are descendants of alsiahas that once lived on your planet. We are harmless just like the descendants, and you will not even recognize them because they look like humans. If we the alsiahas ever come to your earth, our identity will also automatically conform to look like humans, because you are the most dominant species. Einstein, Nostradamus, and Tesla were some of the few humans from your planet who knew that they were descendants because of their genius way of communicating with us on our planet. I hope you did not mean what you said about keeping me from your planet. It won't be like that *Independence Day* movie I told you about. I promise I will come in peace. I was just saying that people would think you were crazier for the reason of building the wall than the actual building of a wall over a planet. That was a good guess about the street sign, but you were wrong. Only the descendants on your earth will be able to see the message in the fiction book made to entertain you humans. I know you, Donald, so don't keep beating yourself up trying to find the message. For one, you're not a descendent, and due to the different forms of alien language, you would be confused. Remember, the book is the best chance for helping me and other aliens get to your earth. You will see that my pen pal ability to write your future life is a gift from AWE and not a lie. I will manipulate letters of words to show you the power of aliens. I'm not a fake psychic like you say. Aliens don't tell the future; we write it. The universe is the source of all connection because of us. I'll show you an example of connection by giving you a little taste of my pen pal ability. I will use the last names of mine and two descendants, Albert Einstein and the first American that orbited the earth, John Glenn. I will even use the first letter of your middle name. I will write where the human that will get credit for my book will be born in 1979, one hundred years after Einstein was born. His first name will be John Glenn's last name. He will have the same last name as mine. He will be born in the state of Illinois. Many people will challenge Einstein's theories. I will write it into existence where a woman will try to challenge the votes of states. She will be denied a recount in a state with the word *pen* in it by a judge who has the letters *P*, *A*, and *L* in his first name. The letter *U* in the judge name will represent universe because of the connection. Her first name will be *Jill*. The *J* in her name will be from your middle name. The *ill* in her name will be from the state her, Glynn, and your opponent will be from. Jill will be nominated by a political party of me and Glynn's last name. I will give her just some of Einstein's last name, just like I replaced the *E* in Glynn's name because I did not want to make it too obvious. Important events in your life will come from the words of my name, *len*, *alien*, *pen*, and *pal*. I'm going to write a man into your life who will be from the same state you're from with a first name similar to the word *alien*. He will be a pro when it comes to predicting the next president. He will pick you as the next president, but not the winner. I will write it where you go to a college with the word *pen* in it. A company with the word *pen* in it will be replaced by your first major real estate deal. Primary houses with the word *pen* in it will exist because of your hard work. You will visit a state with the word *pen* in it while running for president, and there you will propose an act that will end illegal immigration of aliens. This act will be one of many you have planned for your first one hundred days in office if you're elected. Speaking of one hundred, I made similarities between you and the Republican nominee one hundred years before your presidency run. He is from New York like you. His mother shares the same name as your mother. A sister of yours will work in the high courts, like one of his daughters. A sister of yours and a daughter of his will share the same name. I even made it where his vice president running mate and yours will both hold political positions in the same state. The first letter of your first name, *D*, will be use as bait. The defective vice you will complain about after your first presidential debate will not be your vice president, but it will be his first name. The first letter of your last name, *T*, will be used as bait. I will show you our pen pal relationship is not an accidental occurrence. I will replace the letter *D* and *T* in accidental with the letter *P* for the term *pen pal*. If that is not enough pen work from me to prove that my gift is not a coincidence, I will take the letter of your first name from the word *coincidence* and replace it with the letter *P*. The word *pen* will help me choose the last name of your future running mate. I will write it where your vice president pick will be from the same state as the company that will publish my writing. That same state will have my name in it. A judge from that same state will also be written into your life. His middle name will have the letters P, A, and L in them. I will also put the letter U in his middle name to represent university. The judge and your VP pick will attend the same university. The judge will also play a critical role in your university during your run for president. You will find it hilarious to harass the weak. I will turn the word *hilarious* to your political opponent. I will turn the word *harass* around just in case I decide to give you a woman vice president pick. Her last name would also be made from the words of *alien, len*, and *pal*. It will be a president from another country who will also play an important role during your presidency run. *Eureka!* is what you will shout out after discovering his first name. He will have my name scrambled in his first and last name. I hope all this evidence will be enough for you to believe me. If not, I will take the letter of your first name from the word *evidence* and replace it with the letter P. The word *pen* will help me choose the middle name for that president from another country. I will also put the letter A at the end of his middle name to represent *alien*. Your God used Adam's rib to create Eve, and he brought her to him. Just like your creator, I will use letters and words to bring these people to you. All the names I give the people in connection with you will also be the same names I use to find a title for my book. I'm sorry for not liking your song writing, but your bright future won't need those skills. Please write me back, Donald.

From, len

Letter 563 Dec 2 1964

I didn't know aliens had feelings, but let me be Frank with you.

I know I said plenty of times I wouldn't write to you again but this

at this time. No more. this will be my last letter ever to you again so

please do take it personal as I get these things off my chest. This

writing friendship thing we had going has been over for a while,
but of course me not wanting to be rude. I kept it going. you have to
understand my situation. I spill all my secrets and personal

I talk to a stranger I know nothing about for almost ten years. I

know nothing about for almost ten years. As far as I know you

you could be a crazed maniac like that Boston guy they just caught.

The reason that keeps me believing you are a real alien is the weird

way you write. The paper you sent me to write on makes my writing

look different from my normal writing. My writing would be all over the place like pages if I didn't make my own lines. You have no excuse for the way your writing on the paper looks because you're used to it. I don't understand why your planet can't accept our paper. Our clean paper would be like Kryptonite to your dirty planet. Besides your ugly handwriting, your story has a lot of misspelled words with capitalized words in the wrong context. You say its alien law or messaging to write

this way, but I call it a terrible writing. Your pen pal letters don't have that many mistakes like your story you wrote, but its still bad. Nothing about you ... make sense. This ... overall strange writing. Your writing is different in a bad way. this is a clear writing will ... don't write upside down. I thought you guys have schools on your planet. You have the nerve to ask me to represent this thing. Imagine

...me gaining a publishing haze telling an agent that an alien has a

project. Your book to be published because it has a message to call for

aliens on the earth to read. You're not God and I'm no messiah. The best

editor in the galaxy couldn't fix your bad writing. We're a damned smart

I'll g simple. Don't try explaining something if you can't follow the guide-

lines. I won't tell you well good enough that your project is a total

Your alien way of writing is not how we wrote stories here on

earth. Switching writing styles in the middle of a book is something

I've never seen before. I've never seen a novel that consisted of

documents, or a dictionary page. Your introduction is too long and you

should have chapters. It can't be accepted here. We humans write

better than you aliens. Humans on earth who don't know how to

...write stories don't write, we find something else to do. No human being would take time out their lives to read this insane style of writing. I don't believe you aliens know the future like you said. My future life you claim you wrote into existence is a lie and full of of contradictions. It's a direct attack on my life from an alien I thought was my friend. Your future guesses show you are a

desperate attention seeker. Humans don't go this far for attention. The predictions you make are for my future and not the present because you know you wouldn't be exposed. Don't think I'm going to spend my whole life waiting for some false prophecies. The nasty lies you have in this story, about me portrays a person without character. You have me being a bully, a playboy that won't keep a wife, ranting like a wild man on something called twitter. Let's not

forget the awful things you predicted about my wife or as you say

one of my many wives. You said she would be an immigrant and that
the word alien would be ~~immigrant~~ ~~as that~~ scrambled in her first name. I will never forgive

you for that nasty insult. I will say I do think you have things in

this story about me that will be true. I'm sure anybody would

guess that I would one day have more money than my father. I'll be
famous and I will run for president. what does a president from

another country has to do with me or aliens? The connection between

the people in my life during my run for president, and how you will come

up with a book title would be more than a coincidence. It would be

pure attention if it were to come true. I would never look at words the

Same again, stop calling this story a book because its not a book anything but a story. The title of a book has to make sense with what the story is about. You can't get a book title from _____ _____ _____ _____ yourself. Stop thinking you're something important in this world just because there's no 1 in universe. My present or future life isn't ball around world like _____ alien _____ what your prediction

Says you've already convineed me aliens are real, you're not going to convince me to help you come to Earth _____ because of your prediction and made up words. Speaking _____ couldn't _____ come up with another new word calling your name _____. The definition of Immigration is keeping ten and more aliens from coming to my planet. The words _____ _____ and the aliens are really not hurtful, these are actually real words often used on the earth, of course I spelled them a little different, but

who cares. You actually remind me a lot of this student named Lee Alna.

I'm sure you will say you wrote him into my life also. Both of you

guys love making up stories with me involved ??? he also has the word

alien scrambled in his name. So probably the same person or I
mean the same alien. Nightmares about aliens are normal. These

kind of dreams are allowed for a human. You wouldn't understand ???

I was only ten or eleven. I'm a man now and don't have nightmares

anymore. How dare you say I'm scared of you little green monsters. We

just don't want you here because our worlds don't mix. Aliens are different

and happen to humans. You'll just take all space from other humans

being born. The aliens would hurt our females. I don't want ???

...es on earth. That's another new word I made up. You guys would

commit a lot of crimes because of your ignorance to the structure of our

world. You could bring strange odors... you smell worse than

my brother's fart trapped in a glass bottle. I don't believe that aliens are

already here because we're smart enough to know about it. The only

alien thing about Einstein is that weird hairstyle of his. That's

end of you to choose one of the smartest earthlings that ever walked

our planet and try tarnishing his reputation by connecting him to you all.

I really never thought that you would go that far. I don't care about yours

different languages and thank god I'm no alien. I need the story on

my life because you bagged me too, and if a smart person like me couldn't

see a message in the... that obviously mean there's nothing there.

Save your title of names for that Dyrain art when you write their story into existence. Maybe the world ... ... traveling on ... I could care less what you think about the song lyrics. My father and I ... took part in a historical event that ... ... my father ... the building of a wall covering our entire planet to stop you and your friends from entering is every possible after all. By the time you ...

have plans coming to this earth, I'll have enough ... to have a wall built. I'll also be managing my father's real estate ... that I can ... the wall. I'll disguise my real reason with a ... ... another wall until I work my way to the bigger ... It would be terrible if you came to this earth and my friends found out you ... were an alien. My brother ... would be the first ones to

laugh at me. Only god knows what my dad would say. Don't
bother writing to me again. So glad I recieved this letter because
that's not my school anymore. Just in case you don't know, I already
graduated. I have to say the smartest thing you ever did was put
my last name on the map. I hope you keep your promise and scratch
my name out of every single letter we wrote each other. I can't

have none of this stuff tossed back home. Just in case you do make it to earth
please and please don't come in space. This makes a good forever in another
incredible form of the human language from the greatest planet to the
smallest

Letter 563, December 2, 1964

I didn't know aliens had feelings. Let me be frank with you. I know I said plenty of times I wouldn't write to you again, but I mean it this time. No more. This will be my last letter ever to you again, so please do take it personal as I get these things off my chest. This writing friendship thing we had going has been over for a while, but of course, me not wanting to be rude, I kept it going. You have to understand my situation. I spill all my secrets and personal issues to a stranger I know nothing about for almost ten years. As far as I know, you could be a crazed maniac like that Boston guy they just caught. The reason that keeps me believing you are a real alien is the weird way you write. The paper you sent me to write on makes my writing look different from my normal writing. My writing would be all over the place like yours if I didn't make my own lines. You have no excuse for the way your writing on the paper looks because you're used to it. I don't understand why your planet can't accept our paper. Our clean paper must be like kryptonite to your dirty planet. Besides your ugly handwriting, your story has a lot of misspelled words with capitalized words in the wrong context. You say it's alien law or messaging to write this way, but I say it's horrible writing. Your pen pal letters don't have that many mistakes like your story you wrote, but it's still bad. Nothing about you aliens make sense. It's just overall strange writing. Your writing is different in a bad way. This is a clear-writing earth. We don't write upside down. I thought you guys have schools on your planet. You have the nerve to want me to represent this thing. Imagine me going to a publishing house, telling an agent that an alien has a project it wants to be published because it has a message in it for aliens on the earth to read. You're not God, and I'm no Moses. The best editor in the galaxy couldn't fix your bad writing. We're a common-sense planet. It's simple. Don't try explaining something if you can't follow the guidelines. I can't tell you enough that your project is a reject. Your alien way of writing is not how we write stories here on earth. Switching writing styles in the middle of a book is something I've never seen before. I've never seen a novel that consisted of documents or a dictionary page. Your introduction is too long, and you don't have chapters. It won't be accepted here. We humans write better than you aliens. Humans on earth who don't know how to write stories don't write. We find something else to do. No human being would take time out of his or her life to read this insane style of writing. I don't believe you aliens know the future like you said. My future life you claim you wrote into existence is a lie and full of contradictions. It's a direct attack on my life from an alien I thought was my friend. Your future guesses show you are a desperate attention seeker. Humans don't go this far for attention. The predictions you make are for my future and not the present because you know you will quickly be exposed. Don't think I'm going to spend my whole life waiting for some false prophecies. The nasty lies you have in this story about me portrays a person without character. You have me being a bully, a playboy that can't keep a wife, ranting like a wild man on something called Twitter. Let's not forget the awful things you predicted about my wife or, as you say, one of my many wives. You said she would be an immigrant and that the word *alien* would be scrambled in her first name. I will never forgive you for that nasty insult. I will say I do think you have things in this story about me that will be true. I'm sure anybody could guess that I would one day have more money than my father, I'll be famous, and I will run for president. What does a president from another country have to do with me or aliens? The connection between the people in my life during my run for president and how you will come up with a book title would be more than a coincidence. It would be pure alien if it were to come true. I would never look at words the same again. Stop calling this story a book, because it's not. It's nothing but a story, and a title of a book has to make sense with what the story is about. You can't get a book title from people's names. Get over yourself. Stop thinking you're something important to this world just because there's an *I* in *universe*. My present or future life isn't built around words like *Ien* or *alien*, despite what your predictions say. You already convinced me aliens are real. You're not going to convince me to help you come to my earth just because of your predictions and made-up words. Speaking of words, I came up with another new word with your name in it. The definition of *Immigratien* is "keeping Ien and more aliens from coming to my planet." The words I use toward you and the aliens are really not hurtful. These are actually real words often used on the earth. Of course, I spelled them a little different, but who cares? You actually remind me a lot of this student named Lee Ains. I'm sure you will say you wrote him into my life also. Both of you guys love making up stories with me involved, and he also has the word *alien* scrambled in his name. You're probably the same person or I mean the same alien. Nightmares about aliens are normal. Those kinds of dreams are natural for a human. You wouldn't understand, and I was only ten or eleven. I'm a man now and don't have nightmares anymore. How dare you say I'm scared of you little green monsters. We just don't want you here because our worlds don't mix. Aliens are different, and human is normal. You'll just take up space from other humans being born. You aliens would hurt our females. I don't want bialien babies on earth. That's another new word I made up. You guys would commit a lot of crimes because of your ignorance to the structure of our world. You would bring strange odors. I bet you smell worse than my brother's fart trapped under his covers. I don't believe that aliens are already here because we're smart enough to know about it. The only alien thing about Einstein was that weird hairstyle of his. That's sad of you to choose one of the smartest earthlings that ever walked our planet and try tarnishing his reputation by connecting him to you aliens. I really never thought that you would go that far. I don't care about your different language, and thank God I'm no alien. I read the story on my life because you begged me to, and if a smart person like me couldn't see a message in this crap, that obviously means there's nothing there. Save your title of names for that Dyrain girl when you write her story into existence. Maybe she would represent the writing on her life. I could care less what you think about the song lyrics. My father and I just took part in a historical event that's going to shape my future. The building of a wall covering our entire planet to stop you and your friends from entering is very possible after all. By the time you have plans coming to this earth, I'll have enough influence to have a wall built. I'll show you by taking my father's real estate approach that I can build the wall. I'll disguise my real reason with a minor one to build a small wall until I work my way to the bigger wall. It would be terrible if you came to this earth and my friends found out I was pen pals with an alien. My brothers would be the first ones to laugh at me. Only God knows what my dad would say. Don't ever bother writing to me again. Be glad I received this letter because that's not my school anymore. Just in case you don't know, I already graduated. I have to say, the smartest thing you ever did was not put my last name on the mail. I hope you keep your promise and scratch my name out of every single letter we wrote each other. I can't have any of this stuff traced back to me just in case you do make it to earth. Adios, and please don't come in peace. That means good-bye forever in another incredible form of the human language from the greatest planet in the universe.

The lives of Mr. and Mrs. Popsic revolved around their children. They attended all their children's activities in and out of school. If Mr. Popsic couldn't make it, his wife was sure to be there, and vice versa.

The Popsics were, in fact, perfect pushovers. They blamed each other for their kids being spoiled rotten. When the kids had temper tantrums, broke their toys, tormented the neighbors, screaming until their throats went numb—all when young—their parents thought it evidence of high spirits and harmless exuberance. However, now that the kids were older, their behavior seemed far less than adorable. The Popsics tried to put a stop to their obnoxious ways, but it was too late.

They had no favorite among the three children. Love and punishment were meted out with an even hand. Mr. and Mrs. Popsic secretly believed that the only reason they remained married was the children, but they dared not confess it to each other. They would have worked on their marriage if there were not so much urgency in their lives, so much other work demanding attention, or if they had suspected the other's secret concerning the reason for its continuance.

Mr. Popsic had climbed the corporate ladder to become a store manager at Walmart, and few things lit him up with as much self-satisfaction as this achievement. Mrs. Popsic enjoyed the day her husband received his promotion, not because of the increased income but because it gave her otherwise rather insubstantial husband a new confidence. He was diligent about sporting a cleanly shaved face every day, and he never went out anymore with bits of bloody toilet paper on it. For the first time in his life, he took pride in wearing glasses, thinking them a good accompaniment to his newly won status. (In high school, his glasses, and their wearer, had been objects of rather merciless ridicule.)

Mr. Popsic now walked with his squared shoulders high, so high that one might have taken him for the sufferer of a crick in the back. But in truth, he was only bodily expressing his new sense of himself as a giant among men. Mrs. Popsic was more pleased than she might have been over designer elevator shoes. Her husband was only five feet five inches tall, and she now would enjoy a break from his silent despair on the subject.

Mr. Popsic was a couple of inches shorter than Mrs. Popsic, a wound fate had delivered to the tenderest region of his heart (if not missing that organ and hitting his ego). It was such a sore point with him that he actually backed out of their wedding a couple of times. "How," he asked himself frantically, "can I walk down the aisle with a woman who towers over me?" When he was finally persuaded to be married, he hurried the bride at such a pace down the aisle that it looked rather that he was going to tackle the minister before turning on his heels to make a run for it.

Mr. Popsic's sensitivity on this point was enduring, and he seriously considered never having the children his wife so desired out of dread of the day when one or more of them might sprout up beyond the paternal bar he had set at five foot five. Mr. Popsic so badgered his wife on the subject that she struck a bargain with him. They would adopt a Pakistani boy (with the stipulation, upon which Mr. Popsic insisted, that the boy have rickets). Mrs. Popsic, for her part, forced upon her husband the clause by which, after successful adoption of the rickets boy of Pakistan, only natural children, the fruit of Mr. Popsic's loins, would be permitted into the family. Mr. Popsic acceded to this condition only in that it seemed to kick the worrisome can quite some distance down the road, deferring the dreaded happening (of paternal overshadowing) for a very long time.

To the amazement of everyone privy to the bargain struck between the two, an infant with rickets was found in only a matter of weeks, and before Mr. Popsic had time to get his mind around what was now happening (and gain a more definite understanding of what rickets involved by looking it up in *Merriam-Webster's Unabridged Dictionary*), Mrs. Popsic was cooing to a tiny bundle that lay in her arms, displaying a pair of legs stumpy enough to make any father proud.

After his promotion to manager, there was no one in Fremont, California, who could convince him he had ever been five feet five inches in height. Mr. Popsic simply *felt* so much taller that the feeling trumped everything, his recollection of the past as well as his day-to-day experience of reality.

Mrs. Popsic continued as a stay-at-home mom. She was a heavyset brunette partial to buns that she tied up with such force they not infrequently exploded upon her head without warning. At the age of forty-three, she retired from the paralegal profession and took up her passion for sewing full-time. Obsessive-compulsive sewing gave her the freedom to be with the kids and even to withdraw them from the public sphere for homeschooling. She simultaneously discovered that she was very fond of food, of eating food, sometimes in quantities of eating-contest proportions, something that did very little for her figure. In fact, it could fairly be said that she lost her figure altogether as she steadily took on the proportions of a beach ball.

The years flew by, and her seventeen-year-old Pakistani son, Sammy, knew for an absolute fact that he was the luckiest teenager alive. Coincidently, his fourteen-year-old sister, Kamora, felt just the same way. The only child without the cocksureness of a high roller was nine-year-old Jasha, known by her middle name, Olina. Her wheelchair was a constant reminder that at least some portion of the world's allowance of luck had evaded her. However, the Popsics little suspected the truth (perhaps due to a nearly constitutional preference for the fantastic and the foolish): that diminutive, dimple-faced Olina was in fact uniquely gifted. The Popsics allowed her infirmities to blind them to her capacity for love, an endowment without equal anywhere.

The Popsics were quite sheltered, and as such, the love that animated Olina had never been permitted a spreading of the wings. Besides the members of her family, Olina loved some celebrities she had seen on TV and also Tugo, the family dog. Nonetheless, everything Olina turned her love to became a work of power—the sentiment so dominated her character. It was a supernatural attribute from the sky. She had a love that made those in her proximity, usually all unaware as to the cause, gifted beyond the natural trait that makes a person special. Certainly, the forty-seven-year-old Mr. Popsic had no idea Olina was the true reason for his professional achievements, including recognition as employee of the month (month after month) and the numerous bonuses and citations and prizes and, finally, promotion. Mr. Popsic was not one to spread credit for his successes very far, anyway.

Mrs. Popsic had scored her own delicious victory. Her garments were setting fashion trends and were in vigorous demand at the local stores.

No one would have predicted that Sammy would be recruited by the Tar Heel basketball team, let alone that the actual source of his ability was his sister Olina. If Kamora had any inkling of how her video game prowess had been produced by her sister, she surely would have allowed her to win a game once every blue moon. The influence of Olina upon Tugo is hard to estimate with any certainty, for he slept twenty hours out of the daily round of twenty-four, though his dreams seemed quite vivid, as they apparently involved him in pursuits across endless meadows and the kinds of experiences that made him rumble with delight.

May 31, 2031, represented a milestone for Sammy. The afternoon of that day would feature the last basketball game of his high school career, after which he would be off to college. A regular open-gym game at Washington High School brought in over five thousand spectators. Sammy moved with one eye to where he knew his family should be seated, an awkwardness that affected his play not in the least, as he seemed to be everywhere on the court at once. He was a veritable blur in sneakers.

However, the event had begun on a sour note. Sammy couldn't believe that his parents were late for the game. Sammy muttered to himself, "The nerve of them!"

A teammate overheard. "What's wrong, Sam?"

It could be that the question was an innocent one, but Sammy had been on red alert with respect to this young man since learning of his overtures of a few days previous to his girlfriend. Sammy ignored him and his question and returned to ruminating.

Back at the house on 318674 Glencoe Drive, the Popsics were in a mad hurry to make tip-off. Mr. Popsic raced down the hall to fetch some mints for his garlic breath, and he rather blew his top when he stumbled upon his daughters, lost in a video game.

"You stop playing that video game!" he exclaimed in his deepest Walmart voice. "Dyrain, honey!" he shouted (rather as if *Dyrain* had about fifteen syllables in it). "Get the girls!"

Mrs. Popsic screamed for the girls to get ready, finished wrapping food for refrigerator storage, and stepped quickly to Kamora's bedroom, where she found the girls entirely oblivious to the parental warnings (which always had the tendency to make Mr. Popsic's face purple and Mrs. Popsic's face red). Mrs. Popsic put her hands to her hips and raised her voice. She knew that this tactic was doomed, but she knew not what else could be done. So she put the best face on it, as a card player might, and said, "Turn that game off right this minute! You know how late it is!" Mrs. Popsic's meaning was quite clear, but if a horse is not broken young, the risk is run that it never will be, and the young Popsics were anything but compliant.

"All right, Mom," said Kamora. "We just have to wait for the movie part of the game to end."

"Yes, Mother," Olina chimed in. "It is almost done."

Suddenly, an arm reached out over what seemed an enormous distance, rather like the scarf in a magician's sleeve, and Mr. Popsic flipped the game off.

The girls were furious that their father had played the part of a parent and turned their game off while still in progress. Kamora shook her curls in disgust. Olina folded her arms to contain her hard feelings. (Indeed, Olina had been winning, an event as rare as the appearance of Halley's Comet.) But Mr. Popsic wasn't done. No, not yet. After all, he was the manager of an entire Walmart. People listened to him and did exactly as they were told. So he added, "And if you girls don't hurry out and get in the van, I'll shut the game off for a week!"

This specimen of parental firmness was such a trial to Mrs. Popsic's sensibilities that she couldn't bear it; her husband sounded so like a Viking or the boss of the Carlucci gang. "A whole week seems kind of harsh, honey," she purred submissively.

When the girls finally set about getting ready, Mr. Popsic whispered, "My dearest, I think you should go along with me when I put my foot down. They will never take me … that is, never take *us* seriously if we don't back each other up."

"I am sure you are right, darling. It is just that you bring down your foot so hard. It is as if you are smashing skulls with it."

Despite Mrs. Popsic's reservations, the tactic had worked, and the girls were climbing into the family van before even their parents could join them. Olina was carrying on an animated conversation with her wheelchair. "Let's see. Wheels planted, chair stand upright, left wheel into van, right wheel into van, chair returned to original position, strap up. Arg! I can't wait to get a better chair. This is like putting together a set of bookshelves made in Indonesia every time I have to get anywhere in a hurry! All the talking to it that must be done!"

Kamora rolled her eyes. "How will getting a better chair make things easier for you?"

"It will read my mind," said Olina.

"Okay. Now you have gone crazy. Once you have graduated from Poj Rehabilitation Academy, you will never have to use a wheelchair again."

The undetected approach of someone made Mr. Popsic start when he turned and almost ran into him. Dr. Thorgan could see that the family was on its way out, but he refused, in a friendly fashion, to permit Mr. Popsic to leave without a word.

"Not you again," Mr. Popsic said. "I can't talk now. I'm running late." Mr. Popsic was scowling.

"It seems I never catch you at a good time, Mr.—"

The doctor was cut off abruptly with the closing of the driver door of the van.

"Isn't that—" Mrs. Popsic began.

"Yes, it's Dr. Thorgan," Mr. Popsic interrupted.

It irritated Mr. Popsic to watch the doctor's car in the

rearview mirror following behind. If the family weren't seriously late to the game, he'd surely stop the van and drop his severest managerial boom on the doctor, subject him to the kind of verbal abuse that made his employees wither inside. Mrs. Popsic had noticed her husband's indignant distraction. She turned in her seat to get a glimpse of the pursuing doctor, rather blocking Mr. Popsic's view of the road.

Kamora piped, "Look at the spaghetti sauce on Mom's mouth," and she broke into a peal of Olina-induced laughter.

Mrs. Popsic ransacked her purse for a napkin, for she was rather vain on such points.

"What's going on, Sholt, honey?" she finally asked, pursing her lips in the side-view mirror.

"The doctor is loony tunes," snapped her husband. "I don't know what is wrong with him."

Mr. Popsic noticed his wife twice opening the mahort clip on her wedding ring. He knew what was coming next, in that the clip was used only in emergencies.

"No, Dyrain," he cautioned her. "We don't have to get the police involved. I'll handle this guy. I don't know what his problem is, especially today. He never talks to me while I'm in the company of people."

"In the company of people?" Mrs. Popsic groaned. "Since when have you and Dr. Thorgan become friends?"

Mr. Popsic rolled his eyes in disgust. He couldn't believe he had let so much information slip.

"Well, yes, but it was nothing … that is, it was something. It was nothing, but a little something."

"None of what you have said makes sense." Mrs. Popsic frowned.

Mr. Popsic darted a glance at the girls. "I would rather not talk about it in front of the kids." And to Olina, "And get your fingers out of your sister's hair." He was only too glad to change the subject. "Now your sister has to comb her hair all over again. That wasn't nice at all, Olina."

Kamora addressed the back of her father's head. "Dad, my hair is all right. You must have forgotten that Olina does this all the time."

Mrs. Popsic decided to drill him with questions about the doctor later, and Mr. Popsic was relieved to finally arrive at the school. He dropped the family off at the steps of the gymnasium and quickly parked the van.

However, the doctor pulled into the lot right behind and swerved into a parking space nearby. He would make Mr. Popsic meet him. Mr. Popsic tried to scurry into the school, but it was hopeless.

The tall, lanky Dr. Thorgan loomed agitatedly over Mr. Popsic.

"Please, let's talk about this, Mr. Popsic. It is very important that you hear me out."

Mr. Popsic, his face turning quite red, balled up his fist. "If I could reach your face, I'd belt you."

"Please don't feel that way. I have the proof I was telling you about." The doctor held out a sheaf of papers.

His voice rising and falling with emotion, Mr. Popsic replied, "The past couple of times we talked, I went along with your crazy notions. Of course, I never believed you, but I listened, and that should count for something!" Mr. Popsic turned his head as if denying the papers their visibility.

The doctor opened his mouth to explain himself further, but Mr. Popsic presented the flat of his hand.

"You were playing with fire when you talked nonsense about my precious Olina. I listened to you. I didn't get upset. I never called the cops on you. I thought you a harmless nut. And you are nutty! But now you confront me before my family! I will have your license pulled!" Mr. Popsic knocked the bundle of papers from the doctor's hand and walked away with the most withering stare he could muster.

There was nothing for Dr. Thorgan to do but watch Mr. Popsic strut off and to pick up his papers.

Mr. Popsic's righteous belligerence, however, quickly softened in the cheerful atmosphere of the gymnasium. By the time he located his family, his face was so relaxed no one could have guessed what had happened only a moment before.

At the end of the first quarter, Sammy jogged off the court and threw some angry words at his parents. "I can't believe you guys were late. You basically missed the whole first quarter!"

Mrs. Popsic and the girls looked at Mr. Popsic as if he were the guilty party.

"Wait a minute," whined Mr. Popsic.

The second quarter commenced with Sammy making a fancy pass that faked the defense to the opposite side of the ball. The audience cheered from one side and hissed from the other. Against two defenders, Sammy made a three-point shot. He then stole an inbound pass and performed an impressive two-handed dunk. This was turned into a three-point play when he was fouled.

One of the refs joked, "This is supposed to be team play, not the Sammy Popsic show!"

And the game continued in this fashion. Sammy dazzled everyone, including the college scouts who were looking on, desirous of Sammy committing to their schools. The scouts went out of their way to be seen, but talking to Sammy was utterly against NCAA rules.

At the end of the night, Sammy and his team triumphed 106–68.

Later, back at the Popsic residence, Mrs. Popsic prepared the girls for bed.

"Get out of the mirror, Kamora. It's bedtime!" she shrieked.

"May I die my hair scotch blue, Mom?" Kamora brushed her long blonde hair.

"I kind of regret letting you die your hair blonde; you look so pretty as a brunette."

"I don't miss it, but scotch blue is so stylish. People have it like SkijFris, my favorite reality star. Ose Peyha had blue hair in her last video. Blue Ivy even had scotch-blue hair when she was on Broadway." Kamora operated on the assumption that celebrity names would excite her mom.

Olina raised her head from her pillow. "If Kamora can have scotch-blue hair, I can too, right, Mom?"

Kamora raged, "Stop being a copycat, Olina. I said it first."

"Nobody in this house will have blue hair!" Mrs. Popsic exclaimed. She then grabbed the brush from Kamora, marched her to her bed, and tucked her in as if she were a hostage.

"But, Mom! SkijFris has it, and everybody likes her."

"Yeah," Olina chimed in. "We totally love her."

"Well," Mrs. Popsic said, "Skittlefish is a celebrity, and just be glad I'm taking you two to go see her."

"Yeah, in a couple of weeks!" replied Olina with more than a note of excitement in her voice. But both girls thought it their duty to correct their hopelessly unfashionable mother. "Her name is SkijFris, not Skittlefish!"

"Okay, girls. Bedtime. Did you take your vitamin Q?"

Olina frowned as if the experience had not been exactly a pleasure. "Yes, Mom."

Mrs. Popsic knocked on Sammy's door to wish him a good night. She was glad to finally have some time alone with her husband. She went straight to the mirror and took her earrings and contact shades off.

"Today was a good, long day, Sholt." She slipped out of her slippers and plunged into bed. "What was that about the doctor earlier?" she asked.

Sholt was prepared for this very question, so he feigned sleep.

His wife nudged him in the shoulder a bit too forcefully for any romantic interpretation. "Ignoring me, huh? I guess that means good night."

The next morning, Sunday, the Popsic family was awakened earlier than usual by a loud knock at the front door. Instantly awake and as alert as if he had slept in his clothes, Mr. Popsic, assuming that the visitor was none other than Dr. Thorgan, flew furiously out of bed. His wife tried to grab him.

"Sholt! Come back here! What are you doing with that folik?"

If this were not a moment of high drama, mirth being entirely out of place, an objective bystander might have observed that the little furious man clutched the folik in his fist rather exactly as a hungry toddler might his bottle. Bracing for mortal combat, Mr. Popsic gritted his teeth, muttering confidence-building sentiments through them, as he bore down upon the front door. "You want the real Sholt," he could be heard saying. "I'll show you how I do things when I get angry!" The spectacle of Sholt talking himself into courage suggested the metaphysically impossible oscillation of the lion and the lamb, the possibility that at any instant the ostensibly herculean Sholt could dwindle down into a bundle of clothes with just a bit of heat trapped inside. In a gesture worthy of Errol Flynn, Sholt threw back the offending door and squared himself for the fullest possible view of what would have been a barrel chest (were such an appendage possible outside of Sholt's imagination). Sholt, supercharged with murderous assumptions, was rather floored—and, if the truth be known, disappointed—to discover not the doctor but his own estranged father, his father's bubble gum–chewing girlfriend, and her two teenage boys. The father and son, if not for the former's gray hair and rather extravagantly flaunted beer belly, were the spitting image of each other.

"He's in his underpants!" remarked the older boy, choking in laughter.

The comical wealth of the observation was by no means lost on the younger brother, who, for no obvious reason, applied the tip of his finger to the end of his nose and presented Mr. Popsic with the double barrels of his nostrils. The boy's gum-snapping mother, a beauty who seemed not to have spawned teenage sons and moved on but to have somehow gotten trapped in adolescence and undergone shriveling petrifaction in it, couldn't decide whether to stare at Mr. Popsic's face or at his rather bloated midsection.

Mr. Popsic could hardly believe his eyes. How could his father show up at the door like this after their last conversation? Three years had passed, but it was as fresh in his mind as ever. February 9, 2028, was a date he would never forget.

The somewhat trimmer Mr. Popsic had found it necessary to inform his father, "We're in mourning. This is Mom's funeral—you know, your wife?"

"Don't you mean 'ex-wife'?" observed the father.

They had argued in the bathroom of the church.

"You can just throw away all those years you two spent together for some hammerhead of a blonde with a push-up bra?" raged the son.

"You watch your mouth, boy. That hammerhead is soon to be my wife, and you will respect her as such."

"Respect! Where's the respect in bringing her to Mother's funeral? A funeral is where family comes together to celebrate the life of a loved one and to grieve, not make a mockery of the deceased. Jesus H. Christ, that Kewpie doll is just old enough to be your great-grandchild."

"She's part of the family because she's my fiancée. And no one could mistake her for my great-grandchild. Grandchild, perhaps." And this last reflection had illumined his eyes with something not remotely great-grandfatherly.

"I see you're not taking this discussion or the day seriously. I can probably show you what I mean better than I can say it, and it's a good thing me and the rest of the siblings were raised with Mom's last name and not yours." The son had walked out of the bathroom, through the doors of the church, and never saw his father again—that is, until now. And now that father and son had come face to face again, there was the thorny issue of the folik.

"What are you going to do with that folik, son?" The rakish father raised his gray eyebrows in uncertainty. Mr. Popsic was ashamed to have been caught off guard, to have walked into his own trap, and he didn't like feeling vulnerable.

"What an unfortunate surprise," Mr. Popsic said, putting the folik behind him and then, recalling his wardrobe, a pair of briefs, pulling it forward again as if on second thought he had decided to destroy them (rather than merely cover his indecently exposed self). He then slapped on a fake smile, invited the unexpected visitors in, took sixteen giant steps backward with the precision of a rope dancer with a rearview mirror, and disappeared into the bedroom.

Mrs. Popsic was now out of bed and dressing hurriedly.

"Who is it, Sholt?" His wife looked frightened.

Mr. Popsic, papering over his embarrassment with a fraudulently upbeat manner, fixed his glasses to his face with an elaborate show of exactitude and dressed with the deliberateness of one who enjoys the process rather more than seems credible.

"After all this time, he shows himself. His guilt must have been killing him," reflected Sholt.

"Who is it?" demanded Mrs. Popsic rather emphatically.

Mr. Popsic looked up at his wife and displayed a devilish smile. "Pops."

"Mr. Newson? Your father?"

"Yep."

The paternal hammering on the front door had also woken the kids. The girls didn't waste any time getting acquainted with Pop's stepsons. In fact, they got on so famously that the girls invited them to step outside upon completion of breakfast.

The chubby fifteen-year-old boy drew a finger through Kamora's hair and said teasingly, "I bet you I could snatch your yellow hair from your head with one finger."

Kamora drew her head back to free it from the boy's rather grubby finger. "My hair is blonde, not yellow, and I bet I could blow your goofy glasses off with a puff of air."

Olina laughed.

"I know how she could blow your glasses off, Mireol," the younger brother piped. "They would shrivel at contact with her smelly breath."

The brothers high-fived and squealed with laughter.

Kamora, ransacking her brain for a comeback, was eclipsed by her sister.

"My sister's breath never stinks," said Olina, "certainly not as much as your britches do." She then presented the boys with a rather close-up view of her tongue.

Thirteen-year-old Zad, never much of a resource for displays of wit, took another tack, his chubby, freckled face fierce. "How 'bout if I break your cripple chair, eight-year-old smart mouth?"

There was no time for Kamora to step in and interrupt the chain of events. Olina calmly placed her arms on the rests of her chair and said, "Forward six inches."

The next thing Zad knew, he was on the ground and in pain. Olina had rammed him in the knee with an awful thud. Zad yelped in agony.

"You tore my knee up, you crazy cripple!" Zad limped toward the house.

"Hey," said Olina with mock seriousness, "you too can ride in a wheelchair now that your knee is all torn up. You probably wouldn't choose my model—too good for your tastes—but I do have some suggestions. The noxturn chair would be accommodating for a fat boy like yourself."

Kamora placed her hands on her hips and with a backward toss of her head crowed, "Looks like my sister showed you who the boss is."

Mireol's face was so red and clenched in anger that a burning sensation traveled down his body to settle into his sneakers. "If you both weren't girls, I would beat you up!"

"And we would tell our mom and dad," replied Olina.

Mireol was just opening his mouth to respond when Mr. Popsic's voice came screamingly through. "No roughhousing! You be nice to the guests, Olina!"

Mireol wanted to avenge his brother. He imagined games he could invite the girls to play so that he could physically hurt them with impunity. Finally, Mireol said with a smile, "I'll let you girls get a free pass this time. We're old enough to handle this like adults, right?"

Kamora squinted, darting Mireol a distrustful look, and replied, "Yeah. Okay."

Olina shook her head in an unstated agreement with Kamora.

Mireol proposed a game right away, before anyone else could get a bid in. "How about tag? I'll start off as the tagger." Mireol glowed with eager anticipation, thinking this could be the way to get away scot-free with grinding the girls' faces into the dirt.

Olina objected, "That game is played out. I know a better one."

Mireol jumped right in. "Come on, guys! Let's play tag. You guys should be some tough competition." To inspire trust, he injected as much cheer in his voice as possible and patted Kamora on the back.

Kamora couldn't see through his scheme, but she didn't trust him either. "Nah," she said. "I don't feel like running anyway."

"You really wouldn't have to run," said Mireol lamely.

Kamora tried to interject, "I don't think that game—"

Mireol interrupted, "Aww, man! Come on! Let's play tag, and then we can play whatever game you guys wanna." Mireol was growing heated, angry, and desperate, his face waxing fire-engine red.

Olina whispered to her sister, "With a face like that, I don't think we will be playing with him."

Mireol had failed to preserve his brother's honor via vengeance and, angry with himself, he stomped back to the house in defeat.

Olina inquired rhetorically, "You don't want to play our game? Okay. I'd rather play with Sammy than with you Barbie dolls."

Soon the sisters were absorbed in play, so absorbed that they were oblivious to the passage of time, the progress of the sun against the blue vault of the sky, and before they knew it, it was dinnertime. They rushed to join the others at the table.

The competition between the girls and the brothers was still on.

"They're not going to wash their hands?" Zad looked at every adult to make sure he was heard.

Olina frowned at Zad as she zoomed her scholar to the bathroom.

"You too, Kamora." Zad stood, smiled, and pointed toward the bathroom. Kamora knew she had forgotten to wash her hands, but she now refused to in defiance of Zad.

"Go wash your hands, honey," said Mr. Popsic.

Zad and Mireol displayed their most satisfied smiles, making it almost soul-wrenching for her to obey. And for a moment, Kamora held her ground.

"Go!" said Mrs. Popsic impatiently.

"I already did," Kamora lied.

Mireol looked to Mrs. Popsic, waiting for her to command Kamora to the bathroom. Mrs. Popsic didn't. Kamora took the opportunity to furtively display her tongue to the defeated brothers.

"I saw on your CloutCrowd page that you chose the Tar Heels for school. So, do you plan on being at North Carolina for a year before joining the NBA, Sammy?" Pops didn't wait for an answer before extending his jaws like an anaconda over his burger. He swallowed and went on, "You know, you could skip college altogether and go to the ENBA."

Sammy opened his mouth to reply, but he was stopped short by Mireol.

"Kamora's lying! I swear she is! She and Olina came straight to the table without washing. That's why Olina moved so quickly to the washroom when I reminded her." Mireol was bursting with vengeance.

"It's all right, Mireol," Miss Ruso soothed her son.

Mireol, to the innocent observer, was behaving like a certificate recipient from an etiquette school. "No, Mom. Kamora's going to give us all germs, and I refuse to eat if she can't show manners."

"Just go wash," said Mr. Popsic to Kamora.

"But, Dad," Kamora insisted, "I already did."

Mr. Popsic jerked his head toward the humatizer on the wall and said, "What's the big deal? Just go blow your hands."

Kamora finally complied.

The boys eagerly awaited Kamora's reaction when she returned to the table. They scrutinized her face for any sign of defeat but were frustrated by her seeming indifferent. Kamora knew better than to betray any anger. She knew the boys would take that as a victory.

Mr. Popsic picked up his line of reasoning. "My wife and I talked about the ENBA with Sammy. He knows that it has only been in existence for a little while and that it is still in the process of building credibility."

Pops eagerly said, "I just think that with him being Pakistani and all that, playing overseas would be best for him. This boy will make history. He will be the shortest to ever play in the ENBA, the only Pakistani, the youngest, the quickest—"

Mrs. Popsic interjected, "He would be the same in the NBA, but we are more interested in breaking academic records." She smiled at Sammy.

Pops, whose face was red with indigestion, put his burger aside and asked Sammy what he wanted to do. Why, Sammy wondered, would he have to field questions from a grandfather he hadn't seen anytime lately? Sammy put a sour face on and made sure Pops would notice it while answering him.

"I'm okay with college. I heard it was fun." Sammy kept his remarks telegraphic so as to discourage conversation with this man as much as possible.

Pops wanted to continue the discussion and was preparing to pepper Sammy with more questions when Olina spoke up.

"When did you die your hair blonde, Miss Ruso?"

Bereft of a quick reply, Miss Ruso ate on, her eyes suggestive of thought.

Mireol stepped into the breach. "What? You crazy? My mom don't die her hair!"

"Don't be so rude, Mireol," Miss Ruso checked her son. "I don't have to die my hair, honey." She smiled at Olina. "It's my natural hair."

"I thought everyone had natural black hair." Olina looked confused.

Miss Ruso stared Zad down, silently holding him back from further rude remarks.

"Oh, no, honey. People can be born with a variety of hair colors, but mainly black, blonde, and red," Miss Ruso explained to the child.

"What about blue?"

"No, Olina," Sammy said.

"Kamora and I want to get our hair died scotch blue like SkijFris." Olina smiled at Miss Ruso.

"I'm sure there're a million kids that want scotch-blue hair like the reality star SkijFris," Miss Ruso conceded.

"What kind of name is Skisbe?" Pops blurted out.

"Not Skisbe. It's SkijFris," Olina corrected him.

Kamora would also have corrected Pops, but the fries going down her throat prevented her.

"Whatever happened to the kids wanting to dress or look like their favorite sports players or singers? I never thought the day would come when TV reality stars would replace movie stars." Pops shook his head.

"Yeah, it seems to be that way. Back in our day, people worshiped singers, rappers, athletes, and movie stars like you kids do the reality stars of today," Mr. Popsic said.

"I always blamed the fading of the old celebrity on that eqi device," Mrs. Popsic said.

Miss Ruso looked at her boyfriend with a smile and said, "That's what I told you. Do you remember that, honey?"

"Yeah, you did tell me that. You also told me about the overweight singer you posted on your wall." Pops laughed.

"He wasn't fat like that back then." Miss Ruso rolled her eyes.

"No way," Mireol chimed in. "I can't imagine my mom having a poster of a singer on her wall, like Zad has of Rancea Sola." He playfully nudged his brother, embarrassing him.

The girls covered up their mouths in laughter.

"You like older women, yeah?" Mr. Popsic flashed Zad a slight grin.

"Don't believe Mireol. He's fibbing, you guys." Zad couldn't believe that his brother had embarrassed him in front of everybody.

Mireol immediately regretted tripping up his brother and occasioning the sisters' mocking laughter.

"I was just joking," said Mireol.

But this retraction only made things worse.

"Who is the pretty lady on that poster in your room, son?" Pops asked without knowing who she was.

Zad blanched and stammered, giving Kamora a chance

to pounce. "The lady on the poster must be Rancea Sola like Mireol said!" she bubbled.

"What is this, Pick on Zad Day?" The teenager left the table to watch TV, accidently tripping over Tugo, waking him up.

"Kids these days, I tell ya. We pouted over stuff that mattered when I was a teenager, not no wimpy stuff. Teenagers these days are gold fed—spoiled rotten, you are." Pops looked disdainfully at the four youngsters. "Like how it took Zad seconds for his scraped knees to be healed because of the hulka spray. My parents would have washed my knee in water and put a Band-Aid or two on it, and back outside I would go, it maybe taking two weeks for my skin to heal," Pops continued, wielding the past upon the youngsters like a mallet.

"Those times sound scary, Pops." Olina groaned.

"Why do you guys think the eqi is the reason singers are not that popular anymore?" Kamora threw the question out there for any adult to answer.

"I don't know. I just think it is," Mrs. Popsic said.

"Nobody wants to buy tickets for a live show or performance when you can watch it live on eqi. I can just remember when the eqi came out, which was around the time you two were born." Miss Ruso glanced maternally at Kamora and her older son. "At first, the famous people thought this device would be a good idea for making more money. They thought the more the fans saw them on a personal level, the more fans would drool over them and, of course, more money would be spent to watch. Concerts and movie theaters were the first things to take a hit, to suffer sharp drops in ticket sales, but then everything else followed."

Mrs. Popsic joined in, "Yeah, they lost their immortal touch. They should have known that their fans wouldn't be in AWE of them any more once they saw that normal side of them."

"You can see the reality stars twenty-four hours a day on the eqi," observed Sammy, "and it didn't hurt their career. Matter of fact, it helped them."

Sammy thought he had made a valid point until Miss Ruso commented, "They did well because fans expected normality out of them, unlike their superhero athletes and actors or other performing artists. It all started in the early 2000s. First, that Twitter thing that let the fans communicate with the celebrity. Years after that, the teasec helped the fans see their favorite stars' whereabouts throughout the day. That wasn't good enough, so they had to create something that could pry into the normal daily lives of the celebrities twenty-four hours a day." Miss Ruso took a meditative sip from her cup.

"They need to quit selling that device, if you ask me," said Mrs. Popsic, before remembering that she had bought one for the girls.

"I don't understand how a person can watch another person's life all day long," Miss Ruso huffed in disgust.

"The reality stars back in the '90s and the beginning of this century have to be kicking themselves right now for not making the kind of money made today." Pops laughed.

Kamora, who was having a hard time getting a word in edgewise, decided this was a conversation for grown-ups and disengaged.

Mr. Popsic wasn't having much more success. "Speaking of the eqi, my wife and I—"

Pops erupted, "I already know what you're going to say. Sara and I saw the same thing. You were going to mention the husband going to jail when he caught his wife looking at that tennis player on the eqi."

"No, that's not it. You made me forget what I was going to say." Mr. Popsic looked annoyed.

Olina followed Kamora from the table into their room, leaving the others at the kitchen table. Minutes later, Mireol joined them. Mireol's excitement was immediate, and he hollered for his brother. He had seen the girls' PlayStation Infinito XR.

"I can't believe you guys have this," enthused Mireol. "Not only do you guys have the XR, but you guys have the live mode edition. Wow."

"Put it down!" Kamora yanked it from him.

"Whoa," said Zad, trying to grab the PlayStation upon entering the room.

"I hope you guys have clean hands with all this touching you are doing," Kamora teased.

"We can play teams! What kind of games do you have for the PlayStation?" Zad ask.

"You're not playing," Olina declared grimly.

The grown-ups, Sammy included, continued to entertain each other in the kitchen after they were done eating. Mr. Popsic grew increasingly suspicious about his father's motives for visiting.

"I bet you would be a good fit for them Sooners, and the big man Zookasmitchs joining the team could make you guys the best one-two punch in the history of that program, at least since the days of Collier and Randolph." Pops smacked his hand on the table to get everyone excited.

If anyone felt any excitement, Miss Ruso was the only one who showed it.

Mr. Popsic noticed Miss Ruso wasn't wearing a wedding or engagement ring. "I thought for sure you two would be married by now."

Miss Ruso was surprised at Mr. Popsic for touching on that subject. She and Pops had been in a heated argument on that topic just before arriving at the Popsics'. Miss Ruso burrowed her eyes into her gray-haired boyfriend, anxiously waiting for an answer. Pops sat in his chair with a nervous smile, unsure what to say.

He finally let his son know that the hitch was money problems.

"Yes, we won't get married because the money won't let us." Miss Ruso giggled.

Sammy put his head down and quietly chuckled.

Mr. Popsic suddenly suspected why his dad had come over. "So, do you get some kind of money favors for trying to get my son to go to Oklahoma this fall?"

Pops waxed so angry he leaped up out of his chair. Mrs. Popsic told Sammy to go to his room so that he and his father could be alone, and she attempted to tune out their argument by directing her attention to the TV. It was a war of words between the father and son. They criticized each other for about ten minutes. Dr. Thorgan was the only one who could have stopped the father and son from battering each other verbally on that day.

Mrs. Popsic suddenly put her hands over her mouth in shock while watching the news.

"What's wrong?" Miss Ruso exclaimed.

Mrs. Popsic ignored Miss Ruso. Instead, she called for her husband. "Sholt, come look."

Mr. Popsic didn't want to leave his heated discussion, especially in that he was winning the argument.

"It's Dr. Thorgan on the TV!" Mrs. Popsic yelped, waking Tugo up for the second time.

Mr. Popsic was out of the room like a shot. Pops continued

to verbally bash his son while following him out, not caring who Dr. Thorgan was or what the TV was saying about him. Mr. Popsic ignored his father's assault and focused on what was being said about the doctor. Mr. Popsic turned up the volume.

"This is Naras Calit for *On the Spot News*. Today is Sunday, June 1, 2031. Our first story concerns the nervous collapse of Dr. Thorgan, who gained renown for being part of the team of doctors who delivered a record ninety-three babies in one day almost ten years ago at Washington Hospital. Colleagues say it wasn't a surprise. A secretary from the hospital had notified Dr. Thorgan's family members a week before, informing them of the doctor's strange behavior over the past month. The doctor's family and friends said they knew they had to do something when he wouldn't stop singing his favorite song, over and over again, sometimes for as long as five hours straight. Nobody knows the cause of the breakdown, but some think it was stress-related from working long hours. Dr. Thorgan has been transferred to Freemont Hospital until further notice. This is Naras Calit for *On the Spot News*, and we will be right back after these commercials to speak about obesity in America."

"He said this would happen to him if they had a clue he was talking," Mr. Popsic mumbled to himself.

Pops walked around his son to get in front of the TV, to block it from view. Pops's apoplectic face was now a bluish red, and Mr. and Mrs. Popsic ignored him, addressing each other, causing Pops to raise his voice to the rooftop. Finally, Pops yelled for the boys. "Hurry up! We're leaving this place!"

"Oh, come on, Pops! Give us a chance to win a game against the girls. They already won every single game against us today," Mireol whined.

Pops couldn't care less about the boy's complaints or the sour look on his girlfriend's face.

"It's kind of dark. You guys should wait until tomorrow to leave." Mrs. Popsic didn't really care for them staying, but she felt it necessary to show the family that they were still welcome to stay despite the tension.

"No, thanks. Come on, Sara. Let's go." Pops had a firm hold on both boys as they exited. Mrs. Popsic gave Miss Ruso a quick hug before she followed the others out to the car. Mr. Popsic still squinted at the TV, totally unaware his dad had left.

Mrs. Popsic wasn't going to let her husband pull the wool over her eyes again. She wanted to know what was going on, and she wanted to know now. An hour later, at eleven thirty, the couple could be heard in their bedroom arguing over what Dr. Thorgan had or hadn't said.

Sammy flicked on his lamp to search for the earplugs he thought were in his dresser drawer but came up empty. As such, his only recourse was to wrap a pillow around his head. Olina and Kamora were awakened from their sleep. The girls, unlike Sammy, were too curious to return to bed, straining to hear the gist of their parents' argument. Kamora tiptoed into the hallway. Olina used her arms to drag herself to her parents' door and then pressed her ear against it.

"You could have woken the kids with your loud talk, Sholt. And you're still not telling me the truth. I can tell by your empty swallows."

An exhausted Mr. Popsic sat down on the bed and kicked his slippers off in preparation for sleep. His wife sat down next to him, but in such a way as to prevent any lying down.

"Oh, no, not this time! I want to know everything that doctor said, or you will never in life go to sleep again," snarled Mrs. Popsic.

"I'm protecting you from this crazy guy because everything he has said is nuts and makes no sense. What he has to say doesn't matter, and he's gone now, anyway. Trust me on this one, Dyrain."

Mr. Popsic prided himself on his powers of persuasion, but his wife wasn't having any of it. She let him know in no uncertain terms that the prospect of sleep was nowhere in sight.

"We promised each other when we were married that we would be truthful to each other no matter what, and a lunatic doctor is not going to change that," she said.

Mr. Popsic took a deep breath. He saw no alternative.

"Well, you have asked for it. Don't ever say I didn't warn you." Mr. Popsic paused again for another deep breath. "It actually started a few years back. It was then that the doctor approached me with his craziness. He began by hinting about things concerning Olina. I had no notion what he was talking about, until some months ago. He said that there had been too much reason for anxiety to have been more direct, but that now that the time was getting close, he had no choice but to spell everything out. Do you really want to hear this story, honey?"

Mrs. Popsic merely folded her arms and stared daggers into her husband.

With visible reluctance, he continued. "Do you remember the secret space expedition in December 2012 that I told you Dr. Thorgan had informed me of? It was when every person thought the world was going to end or something."

Mr. Popsic waited for a response, but his wife only sat as still as a park statue, her arms crossed. "Well, the doctor tells me that some debris was removed from the shuttle after its return to Earth. NASA passed it along to a special team of scientists for analysis. After testing the debris against materials from all other known planets, an identification could not be made, and the mystery remains to this day. I can't believe I still remember what this nut told me. Now I feel like the stupid one." Mr. Popsic smacked his forehead with the flat of his hand.

"Go on," Mrs. Popsic urged.

"After freezing the fragments from space, as requested by the president of the United States, the lead scientist, Hysal Muke, secretly retrieved it ten years after the discovery, around the time Olina was born in 2022. This is where it gets interesting, honey." Mr. Popsic stood up with a wry smile. "Hysal experimented with the materials in one of his many secret lab locations, and this lab was a block from the hospital in which Olina was born that twenty-seventh day of December. Hysal heard the news of all the babies being born and wanted to be part of history himself, and so he went to the hospital. He helped the doctors there with the delivery of a record ninety-three babies, not realizing that he was toxic. This, Dr. Thorgan claims, is the reason these children became ill."

"Everybody knows it was that cold wind that seeped through the cracked window in the hospital basement," said Mrs. Popsic, finally putting her hands on her lap.

"So you do believe it's gibberish talk?"

"Of course, but that doesn't mean I want you to stop talking about it."

"The scent of the substance was too strong for the newborns to inhale, and that's why every single one of them became disabled in some kind of way. Dr. Thorgan says Olina has developed some kind of special power because she was the only one held by Hysal, vastly increasing her exposure. Dr. Thorgan had an answer to every question. When I asked him how he could know that Hysal held Olina, he said it wasn't hard to recall the shortest man in the room with tears of joy in his eyes standing next to Hysal."

Mrs. Popsic covered her mouth to stop herself from laughing out loud.

"I guess you don't want to hear the rest?" Mr. Popsic asked, agitated.

"I'm sorry, Sholt. Please continue."

Mr. Popsic hesitated.

"I said I was sorry. Now finish up," said Mrs. Popsic rather sternly.

"I asked him how he would know about this so-called power. The nut said that Hysal and a team of scientists tested the space debris on rats and that it made them ten times stronger than a fifty-pound dog. A rat stronger than a dog! Come on!"

The Popsics laughed.

"I told Dr. Thorgan that was where his logic went all screwy. Olina isn't strong at all. She doesn't even have the strength of a normal kid her age. Hysal's team of scientists didn't make any positive discoveries concerning the children, but Dr. Thorgan remained suspicious and decided to investigate the matter himself. That's why the rehabilitation school has been built by Hysal Muke, and that's why Dr. Thorgan wants us to remove Olina from Poj Academy. Dr. Thorgan said Hysal's goal is to find out if any of the kids were affected by the debris, and if so, he wants to use them for his evil purposes. Crazy man even said the reason Aurora, Illinois, was chosen for the location of the school is because his favorite movie, *Wayne's World*, was made there. God, he would ramble on and on."

Mr. Popsic paced the room as if the effort to remember Thorgan's words were aerobic.

"Is that all, Sholt?"

"Oh yeah! I remember. The doctor said conducting his own personal investigation revealed that Olina was the only one of the children who had acquired special powers. He said that it was Olina's love for us that made us succeed and achieve good things, and that this influence could be reversed—that it could make people quite evil, capable of horrendous behavior. He claimed he had much more to tell me, but when he appeared in front of you and the kids—that was it! He had crossed the line! When he caught me in the parking lot at the game, he claimed that Hysal was trying to 'get rid' of him out of fear of what he knew, out of fear that he might talk. I tell you, this Dr. Thorgan is a menace. I am sure he would have gone on and tried to persuade me that Olina is a wizpire." Mr. Popsic hung up his robe on the back of the door and kicked his shoes to the side before climbing into bed.

The girls were still outside the door, trying to catch every word.

"Except for when Dad walked by the door, I could hardly hear what he was saying," whispered Kamora to Olina as they crept back to their bedroom.

"I heard the part where Dad said I was a wizpire," Olina said, lifting herself into bed.

"Yeah, I heard him," Kamora confirmed.

The girls stayed up for a while to chat excitedly about watching the movie *Half a Howl* to learn more about Olina's newly disclosed nature. The night couldn't fly by fast enough for them. The girls usually stayed in bed until about eight in the morning. Previously, only Christmas Day could rouse them at six. But on Monday, June 2, six o'clock found them riffling through the collection of VMs in the living room, determined to find a copy of *Half a Howl*. Mr. Popsic didn't notice the girls as he moved through the house, getting ready for work.

"Got it!" Kamora shrieked, the VM held high in her hand.

Mr. Popsic walked from the bathroom, a toothbrush jutting from his mouth as he neatly knotted his tie. He mumbled something unintelligible and returned to the bathroom. Olina slid the movie into the codar.

The two were all attention, especially when the wizpire appeared.

"I am surprised you girls are up so early," said Mr. Popsic, glancing at the movie. Getting no response, he left for work.

"If I am toxic like the wizpire, I should be able to do what she does," Olina mused aloud.

Kamora said nothing. She was too absorbed in the movie.

Finally, Kamora remarked, "It would be amazing if you could do the things the wizpire does."

Olina wanted to put the movie on pause so that she could conduct some tests of the state of her powers. But Kamora put a hand to her wheelchair, preventing her from stirring.

"Relax, Olina. The movie's not done yet."

"Let's go outside and see if I can do that stuff," Olina enthused.

"Wait until the movie is over. Besides," noted Kamora, "you won't be able to find out until nighttime and the appearance of the moon."

Twenty minutes later, the movie came to an end. The girls proved beyond any shadow of a doubt that no one alive could care less about the history Mrs. Popsic had made the subject of a quiz.

Olina couldn't resist the urge to move her head from side to side, just as the wizpire had while dodging dangerous spheres in her flight through the forest. Tugo even entered into the spirit of things by wagging his tail and slobbering a great puddle onto the carpet. Kamora began acting out a scene when Mrs. Popsic broke off her lecture and glared at the two over her reading glasses perched at nose end.

"I can well imagine that you two are upset to be taking the final test, but you have to stay focused nonetheless."

Kamora frowned deeply before returning to her history book. The girls knew that they would have to exercise patience if they were not to tip their mother off to their plans for later on. It required enormous effort, but they managed to stay focused on history until the lesson was over.

Mrs. Popsic began cooking dinner, and in a couple of hours, it was brought to the table. Mr. Popsic had put in overtime and seemed in a desperate hurry to get to the tuna salad casserole.

"Sholt, you are supposed to eat the salad first," Mrs. Popsic chastised.

Mr. Popsic ignored her, merely stuffing more food into his mouth.

"Girls! Dinnertime!" Mrs. Popsic sang out as she seated herself. She would have called for Sammy, but she remembered that he was at a friend's house. The girls had little interest in dinner given what lay before them that evening.

"Kamora! Olina! I said to come and eat your dinner!" Mrs. Popsic now had a note of irritation rising in her voice. When the girls finally presented themselves, irritation turned to aggressive suspicion when she sighted a white substance on Olina's ear.

"What's that on your ear?" the mother asked.

"Nothing but lotion," Kamora said with a bit too much force, quickly wiping it away and then flashing a timorous smile.

"You girls have been acting strangely all day. I wonder if it is because Sammy is leaving," Mrs. Popsic speculated somewhat hopefully.

"I am going to be sad when he leaves," Olina confessed with downcast eyes.

"Don't worry, dear. We will be able to talk to him anytime we like, and we get to see him practice live on eqi," Mrs. Popsic consoled.

That reminded Olina of the new school she would be attending in August.

"I'm glad I don't have to go all by myself to Poj Academy," Olina observed.

Kamora interjected heatedly, "I still don't think it's fair that Sammy and Olina get to experience a real school while I am stuck at homeschooling. On top of that, I have to move hundreds of miles away. Why can't she just go by herself?"

"Now don't be selfish, Kamora. The move to Illinois is only temporary," Mrs. Popsic remarked.

Mr. Popsic shook his head in agreement with his wife and ate on as she continued.

"We all have to go. It isn't just you. I'm sure that your father would like to stay at the Walmart here, with all his friends and a comfortable work environment, rather than transfer to the Walmart in Aurora, Illinois. But it's called sacrificing for your loved ones. Just think of the other families that also have to move out of the state so that their kids can attend the academy," Mrs. Popsic finished.

AWE Narration

*T*hat's a better way to tell the story, fifteen-year-old Dyrain thought to herself after reading the last page. It had begun as a mere document, but Ien made it into a story. She didn't expect it would be that interesting. Otherwise, she would have told her pen pal, Ien, to send her the entirety of the story. After reading the story, her parents returned home, where she quickly reminded them of her practice drive.

Dyrain ran out to her parents in the parlor with a driver's permit in hand. "Can you guys take me for my drive? Can I drive today?"

Mr. Phelps walked past his daughter without saying a word.

"Your father and I are tired. You know we had to do the station by ourselves today." Mrs. Phelps frowned.

"What about later?" Dyrain asked somewhat tearfully.

"Maybe after we get some rest. Don't you have homework to do?" Mrs. Phelps asked.

"Summer school ended a few days ago. The driving permit is our only homework," Dyrain said exasperatedly. Dyrain angrily threw the permit down onto the floor. She had been turned down for the third time in a week.

"We're tired. Oh, no, we're busy. Not today. Maybe tomorrow," Dyrain mocked her parents with rage simmering in her low voice before storming off.

This was one of the many times Dyrain ran up against the disadvantages of being an only child. She could have used someone to talk to like her best friend, Cindy, but Cindy was visiting family out of town. If only she could call Ien, with whom she had been exchanging letters for five years. However, Ien had been forbidden to provide her his phone number. Reflecting upon her five-year friendship with Ien and the fact that she had never heard his voice or seen his face seemed nuts and did nothing to brighten her mood.

"I don't need cheering up. I need to be checked into a mental institution," she said to herself as she grabbed her pen pal album from the closet shelf. Bored and upset, Dyrain turned to one of her favorite diversions when time was heavy on her hands. She began a new letter to Ien, stopping at intervals to read her pen pal album, which consisted of saved letters from Ien and herself, along with the original and new document Ien wrote. Many letters remained even though she had had to destroy many of them upon being caught in the act of perusing them by her parents. She first reread some of the original document on her life Ien had sent her, the one that had promoted her to encourage him to compose the same material in the form of a story for a new document, a story so far that's turning out to be better than the original document.

2000/ Jan 16

Dyrain's Original Document

Days Date>May 31>Year 2031>Day (Saturday)
FATHER (Sholt Popsic) AGE (46) HEIGHT (5'5")
LBS (139) EYE COLOR (Brown)
HAIR COLOR (Black)
RACE (Caucasian) DOB (August 3, 1984)

Days Date> May 31 > Year 2031> Day (Saturday)
MOTHER (Dyrain Popsic) AGE (45) HEIGHT (5'7")
LBS (185) EYE COLOR (Brown)
HAIR COLOR (Black)
RACE (Caucasian) DOB (May 22, 1986)

Days Date> May 31 >Year 2031>Day (Saturday)
SON (Sammy Popsic) AGE (17) HEIGHT (5'2") LBS (135)
EYE COLOR (Hazel Brown) HAIR COLOR (Dark Brown)
RACE (Caucasoid) DOB (March 25, 2014)

Days Date> May 31 >Year 2031>Day (Saturday)
DAUGHTER 1 (Kamora Popsic) AGE (14) HEIGHT (5'4")
LBS (129.5) EYE COLOR (Brown) HAIR COLOR (Black)
RACE (Caucasian) DOB (February 4, 2017)

Days Date> May 31 >Year 2031>Day (Saturday)
DAUGHTER 2 (Olina Popsic) AGE (8) HEIGHT (4'7")
LBS (63) EYE COLOR (Light Blue) HAIR COLOR (Black)
RACE (Caucasian) DOB (December 27, 2022)

The SON was out of bed at 8:04 a.m. DAUGHTER 2 was out of bed at 9:19 a.m. The MOTHER was out of bed at 9:34 a.m. DAUGHTER 1 was out of bed at 10:07 a.m. The FATHER was out of bed at 10:40 a.m. The SON entered the bathroom at 8:04 a.m. DAUGHTER 2 woke DAUGHTER 1 up at 9:19 a.m. The MOTHER retrieved one of her slippers from underneath her bed at 9:36 a.m. DAUGHTER 1 entered the bathroom at 10:08 a.m. The FATHER put his robe on at 10:41 a.m. The SON gargled at 8:06 a.m. DAUGHTER 2 entered the kitchen at 9:21 a.m. The MOTHER entered the kitchen at 9:38 a.m. DAUGHTER 1 sat on the toilet at 10:13 a.m. The FATHER used the telephone at 10:42 a.m. The SON flossed his teeth at 8:07 a.m. DAUGHTER 2 ate a bowl of cereal at 9:28 a.m. The MOTHER cleaned up DAUGHTER 2's mess at 9:42 a.m. DAUGHTER 1 took a shower at 10:19 a.m. The FATHER knocked on the bathroom door at 10:53 a.m. The SON brushed his teeth at 8:08 a.m. DAUGHTER 2 knocked her bowl of cereal off the table and onto the kitchen floor at 9:35 a.m. The MOTHER ate spaghetti left over from last night at 9:52 a.m. DAUGHTER 1 dried herself at 10:41 a.m. The FATHER picked up the newspaper from the front porch at 10:55 a.m. The SON washed his face at 8:11 a.m. DAUGHTER 2 screamed for her MOTHER to help her clean up the cereal and milk at 9:35 a.m. DAUGHTER 1 smilted her hair at 10:45 a.m. The FATHER warmed up food in the blazet at 11:15 a.m. The SON dried his face at 8:13 a.m.

1996/December 2

Dear Dyrain,

My name is Ien Green, and I'm writing you because our
school said we had to find somebody to write to, and my
teacher chose you for me. Can you please write back? You
can send your letter to 13050 Oak St, Wheatland, Wyoming.
Hope to hear from you soon.

 Dear Ien,

*My name is Ruth. I am Dyrain's fifth-grade teacher. When you write
Dyrain next time, could you send your school information with the
name of your teacher?*

Sincerely, Ruth

Letter 3

1996/December 28

Dear Ien,

My name is Dyrain Phelps. I'm the girl you wrote almost a month ago. I didn't know what a pen pal was until a friend told me. I would have written you sooner, but my nosy teacher locked your letter in her drawer after she read it to me. When she left her drawer open a couple of days ago, I was able to peek inside and get your address. She didn't want me to write you back because she said it was strange for you to give me an address that wasn't for a school. How old are you? What school do you go to? Write me at my house address and not the school. I can get the mail before my parents get off work. My babysitter brings it in, but she just puts it in my parents' room. My address is 1037 North Avenue, Santaquin, Utah. Just in case you need my ZIP code, it's 84655.

Your friend, Dyrain

Letter 4

1997/January 7

Dear Dyrain,

I'm really happy you wrote me back. I didn't think your teacher would give you such a hard time. My teacher is the one who picked out kids from schools throughout the country for pen pals. I'm ten years old, and I go to Washington Elementary. I am also in the fifth grade. I'm an only child. My dad takes care of me since he and Mom broke up. I also didn't know what a pen pal was until my teacher told me. I don't think any of the other students knew what a pen pal was. Elsa and Matthew said they knew, but I didn't believe them. My teacher said this pen pal thing won't be graded. "This project is aimed at expanding your minds. This will open your mind to another world," he says. I think he's lame and funny. I hope it doesn't bother you that I don't address the letter correctly. If it does bother you, I can fix it.

Hope to hear from you soon.

Letter 5

1997/January 13

Dear Ien,

You don't have to worry about fixing the letter. I think it's good. I can't believe that you're the only child. I am too. I am also ten, and I do have one sister, but she never made it out my mother's belly. I bet you are bored like me because you're the only child. A bunch of times, I am glad to be the only one because all the Christmas toys go to me. I just don't have anybody to play with regularly. My stupid teacher told my parents about the first letter you wrote. My dad made a fuss over it and warned the teacher that he would call the police if it happens again. Grown-ups are strange, if you ask me. My parents are the meanest people alive. If they found out I was still getting letters from you, they would ground me for life. I'm glad I'm your pen pal. Write back soon.

Your friend, Dyrain

1998/June 7

Dear Dyrain,

You are so hilarious, girl. I must have laughed the whole time I was reading your letter. Who would have thought your school play was going to end like that, with Jim choking on the dog's bone and going to the hospital? Laura was the reason, don't you think? Just think about it, Dyrain. If Laura would have agreed with Jim about which food is healthy for the dog, Jim would never have had a reason to put Fata's bone in his mouth. I'm sure they can find somebody else to take Jim's place since it's only a school play. Are your parents still mad over the expensive china you lied about breaking? How could you blame it on an old couple like the Andersons? You should have told them a better lie like blaming it on your troublemaking neighbor, Phillip. I'm doing better in my science class now. My D turned into a B. I had to do better in science if I didn't want to go to summer school. I heard a rumor that they were going to do a remake of Knight Rider *and that the car would be white instead of black. I don't know if that's going to work. Do you watch reruns of* Knight Rider*?*

Write back soon.

Letter 34

1998/October 22

Dear Ien,

I'm sorry that it took me three weeks to respond to you. You're not mad, are you? It's Mr. Big Belly's fault. He gave us a research paper and a take-home test. I was so tied up. I still probably could have squeezed some time in there to write you, but my parents also had me helping them at the gas station all freaking week. I could have called you, but you won't give me your phone number. I slipped up and said your name when I was talking to Cindy the other day. It was a good thing she wasn't paying attention. I don't know how I would have played that off. My parents ended up giving the puppy away that I found in the backyard. Actually, they located the owners in an ad for the missing dog in the newspaper. You forgot to tell me how I looked in the pictures I sent you. Do you like my hair better short or long? I know you told me you won't send a picture because my parents or somebody could find it, but I promise that won't happen if you send me just one. Will you think about it? At least I would stop thinking that you're probably some old fart who likes little girls.

Your friend, Dyrain

1999/July 10

Dear Dyrain,

What's up, friend? How are you today? I'm all right. Just got back from swimming. And plan on going to the neighbor's barbecue in a couple of hours. Never mind what I said the last time; I was just joking. I really wasn't joking, but I just didn't mean for you to get upset over the alien talk. I hope I didn't lose your trust over the truth. Sorry I don't have much to say today. I'll have more to say next time I write you.

Your frIENd

Letter 85

1999/September 2

Hey, Ien, I sent you Jessica Andrews's Heart Shaped World *CD like you asked me. I still think LeAnn is a better singer. You owe me big-time because I had to pay $3.50 to get it mailed. Cindy is still not talking to me. It's now gonna be three weeks and a half she hasn't said anything to me. I saw her staring at me in the lunchroom. It looked like she was ready to talk to me. I quickly turned away and walked the other way on purpose. I want her to suffer for taking so long to be my friend again. I'll probably say something to her next week if she doesn't give in and speak to me. I would have talked to Cindy if she wasn't hanging around that Judy girl I despise. Bringing up Jessica again, you still never gave me the details of Jessica's concert you went to at the Grand Ole Opry. Write back and don't forget to send my money.*

Your friend, Dyrain

1999/December 23

Dear Dyrain,

What is my best friend doing? No, I'm just playing; I wish you were my best friend. At least I could call you my best pen pal friend since Cindy is your one and only best friend. I couldn't wait to tell you about the crazy dream I had. It was a fight at school between Ryan and Jay, but in my dream, Ryan's name was Amerigo, and Jay's name was Ulysses. Amerigo and Ulysses were both suspended after a big fight between the two of them. It started because Nya sat next to Ulysses on the bus during a field trip to the zoo. Amerigo thought that Nya was still his girlfriend since she never told him to his face that she had broken up with him. Amerigo snatched Nya's backpack from her so she could leave Ulysses to sit with him. That idea backfired on Amerigo because she told the teacher on him and made him give it back. Ulysses laughed at Amerigo and called him a loser. Amerigo swore revenge. When we arrived back at the school from the zoo, Amerigo jumped on Ulysses right away. It was tough for the teachers to break the fight up due to the students surrounding the fight. It was total mayhem. I have never seen a fight last that long. In the end, both were losers. Amerigo came out the biggest loser because he lost the fight, and Nya was suspended along with him and Ulysses. The next day I saw Nya and Christopher walking in the hallway holding hands. That Nya girl is a true heartbreaker. Write back soon.

Your frIENd

Letter 130

2000/August 2

Dear Ien,

You're not going to believe this, but you have to send me the same letter, if that's possible, since you said it was so important. I had to rip it up or else my mom, who came home early, would have caught me. I'm really sorry.

Hope you can do it.

2000/August 17

Dear Dyrain,

It's not easy for me to send you the same exact letter. Not everyone makes copies of their own letters before mailing them off and turns them into a pen pal collection like you, Dyrain. I know my handwriting is not the best, but I didn't think that was a cause for you to type our pen pal letters, your future story, and the documents out. Who does that? That's beyond dangerous. What if your mom would have decided to search your whole room after she saw you rip up some of the letters? This is like the fourth time you've almost been caught. I know I said I would do you any favors if you read your life story, but that didn't mean for you to be so risky. I hope you really didn't lie about ripping it up just because you don't want to hear what I have to say. I hope you will take me seriously and not ignore me like last time when I sent you the document. Please take this letter here seriously. It's the truth. Even if you don't believe me, please still be my friend afterward. I have mostly told you the truth about me from the time of my first letter until now. What I kept from you at the time was for a good reason because I needed to gain your trust first, and I think our four-year friendship did that. I should have given you more information before I sent you some of your life document the first time. I'll just give you a little information for right now because I don't want to overwhelm you. Every human's life in the world is manipulated to what us aliens want it to be from the time the human turns twenty-one. We've been doing this since the caveman times up until Hysal's great-grandfather, who was a scientist, found a way to us in 1891. When he died, his son took over, and after his death, his son Hysal Muke inherited us. Hysal, like his father and grandfather, has been using aliens to manipulate for him since 1958. Yes, aliens do exist, but not as you humans think we are. We don't fly in UFOs. We don't look like monsters, and we are not from mysterious planets. All those lies and false sightings were set up by Hysal's great-grandfather Vrokma to insult the aliens. He did it out of revenge for us manipulating the humans for millions of years. Hysal is now doing the same exact things for revenge. Hysal even tried brainwashing us, telling us he was the one who created us for the purpose of taking the humans' place on earth. His lies and plans were cut short when we found out that he discovered a way to get rid of us. We began to think of ways to escape. By that time, he had gained access to our pen pal ability to control the human life himself, something his father and grandfather weren't able to do. Hysal already had 86 percent of peoples' lives documented after he intercepted it from the aliens' minds, and he figured that was enough for what he had planned. You were one of the people's lives he couldn't get because my dad and I escaped. Each alien possesses the pen pal ability to document one human being's entire life after the human is twenty-one. I have the documentation to your life. My dad has the documentation of Alvin Owen's life that was already taken from him by Hysal a month before the escape. Since aliens don't have souls, my dad and I will live forever unless Hysal finds us. The secluded building in Russia we were in is the same building the aliens who were captured by Vrokma stayed in. I'm sure that's the same building Hysal is still working in to this day. I'm able to know this past information about my aliencestry because of a notebook full of alien history my dad stole from the building before *our escape and also because the older aliens who were in captivity with us gave us some information. Hysal thinks he got rid of all the aliens, but my dad and I and a handful of other aliens were lucky enough to escape due to a miscount by his staff. We were able to escape from Russia and move to the United States. We blended in with the humans without suspicion because of our ability to conform to the identity of you guys. It was never my teacher's idea for this pen pal stuff. He knows nothing about it; nobody does, but me and my dad. The truth is, I am your pen pal, but not the pen pal defined by you humans or, should I say, by Vrokma. Vrokma gave our pen pal ability a new definition upon his takeover. In alien terms, a pen is used to write a human's life into existence. That makes the human and alien forever connected; the two words pen and pal come together as one representing both the alien and the human. I'm not allowed to tell you the first and last name my dad gave me after our escape, but Ien is the name our supreme leader gave me. Aliens don't have last names like humans. Not allowed to use the last name I use for school, my dad let me have a second last name for the pen pal letter writings. My dad and I chose the last name Green since that's the typical color aliens are known to be to you humans. The address you write to me is real, but it's not where my dad and I live. We have a way of getting our mail before the real people that stay in the house get theirs. I hope you understand why I had to lie to you. It's for me and my dad's own protection. I had to think of some kind of way to contact you. My dad didn't think it was a good idea at first for me to write you. It took him a few years to get tired of me constantly nagging him that your life is going to one day save both the aliens and humans from Hysal. My dad even proofreads my letters just in case I give you too much or too little information. We aliens coming* together gives us the strength to take our power back from Hysal Muke. Once you read your entire story I send to you bit by bit, I think you will begin to understand the importance of all this and most of all become a believer in the alien race. I just can't believe I get to document the girl's life that will one day bring us aliens back together and stop Hysal from getting rid of the human race.

Your frIENd

Letter 206

2001/July 9

Dear Ien,

I want to start this letter off by thanking you for your advice about Charles. Thank you for always being my friend when I need you. I know you get tired of hearing about my problems with my parents or about Cindy and other girly problems. Either you are a bored individual who loves to write or you really do care about me like you say. I really do thank you for listening to me. Your advice seems to be shady sometimes, like when you told me to stop being friends with Cindy for good because she threw yogurt in my face. I understand you were upset and just looking out for me, and that still made me appreciate you all the more. I guess you can call this an appreciation letter. Believe me when I tell you this letter was in the making and not a spur-of-the-moment thing. I love you so much as a friend, I want to prove it to you, and I promise I won't talk about Charles again. I don't care if I ever see that boy again. It's no big deal to me. As far as I'm concerned, he doesn't exist in my mind. Enough of him. I know you're going to be surprised when I say this because it's been over a year since I ignored what you had to say about aliens, but you can send me a document again as long as it's in story form, because the first document you sent was confusing. It must be an alien thing to have the time included in every sentence because I just don't get it. I promise I won't mock or make fun of you like the last few times you tried telling me about your alien life. You have my word, Ien. Whatever you want me to do to help, I will do it.

Your friend, Dyrain

Letter 207

2001/July 27

Dear Dyrain,

My dad and I jumped for joy when we read your letter. This is what I've been waiting for. I'm so happy right now to even care about how you ignored what I had to tell you last year. As long as I have your word, I know you will do right by my side. The first thing I'll do is send you some of your life story I put in story form to see if you will like that better. I'm really excited, and yes, I used that grammar and punctuation book you sent me. I also read a few short novels to get an idea of how to put the document in story form so you can understand it better. I'm curious to know what you think. Please hurry and write back.

Your pen pal, Ien

Letter 208

2001/August 8

Dear Ien,

You have no idea how I feel right now. My parents won't take me for my practice drive. If I knew I wasn't going to be able to drive, I would have just waited to take my driving class in the fall instead of going to some stupid summer school. They told me when I got my driver's permit that I could practice anytime I wanted. Now that I've had it for a week, both of them have been making a million and one excuses. I'm so angry right now; I could walk into their room right this minute and tell them how I feel. I bet when you turned fifteen and got your permit, your dad took you for your practice drives without making lame excuses. With all the weird things you tell me about you and your dad, he probably doesn't know how to drive himself. Do aliens drive? No, I'm just joking. You don't have to answer that, but I am kind of curious. Well, enough of that talk. Even though I think this is the craziest story ever, I think this story is better than the first one you sent in documentation form, and of course I still don't believe it will happen, because nobody knows the future. You spelled the word die *wrong more than a few times. It's supposed to be spelled* dye. *I tried fixing it but couldn't erase it or write on the paper—how weird. You don't have to put the actual date every time it's a new day, and you didn't have to capitalize the word* awe. *Those Twitter and eqi device–type things would never happen. No celebrities will let people get into their personal lives like that. That's called stalking, and yes, you will go to jail for that. It's bad enough that they have to deal with the paparazzi. There are a bunch of things in your story that you got wrong about me. The fat jokes about me are not funny at all; it's rather rude. I would never be a fat, out-of-shape woman or marry an insecure, short man. The only person I would ever marry is my crush, Gary Hortan, and even though he is a senior and I am a freshman, he will wait for me. You could have come up with a better last name than Popsic. Have you ever heard of somebody with that last name? Sholt's dad's name shouldn't be Pops because it's so close to Popsic and that's confusing. The crazy idea of adopting a baby because of height issues and having rickets is just ridiculous. I know you're trying to impress me with your big words and all, but please make the writing simple. Just be yourself. I'm not going to hate you because you don't put those dictionary words in my story. Mr. Popsic isn't the only one who has to look in the* Merriam-Webster *dictionary. Of course I'm not a stupid person, but I'm tired of looking in the dictionary for the meaning of words like* mirth *or* exuberance *or trying to figure out what sentences like the* metaphysical *oscillation of the lion and lamb mean. I do enough of that in school. You can also keep those words you made up out of the story, or just change the whole story again. If that man Hysal Muke is such a bad guy, why would you put him in my life story? And even if this whole farce is true about saving the humans and aliens from Hysal, the aliens would still be seen as the lesser of the two evils since you guys would let the humans live, or so you say.*

Sincerely, Dyrain

AWE Narration

Dyrain fetched her stamps from the closet to put on the envelope after she enclosed the letter. She headed out of her room, past her parents' room, to mail the envelope, but she quickly turned back to her room when she saw her mother in the kitchen preparing dinner.

"Where are you going?" Mrs. Phelps asked.

It was a good thing Dyrain saw her first; otherwise, Mrs. Phelps would have seen the bright yellow envelope in her daughter's hand. Dyrain was quick enough to slip the envelope into her shorts, but she was too slow to disappear out of her mom's sight. Dyrain didn't want her mother to become suspicious. She decided again to go outside since her mom had already seen her with her shoes on.

Dyrain gasped. "Oh! I thought you were asleep, Mother. I'm just going outside to get some fresh air for a little bit."

Dyrain was surprised her strict mother didn't have any more questions for her before she was able to make it outside. Usually, it was the neighbor's dog barking and jumping that frightened Dyrain when she made her way to the corner mailbox. Now her mom would be another obstacle to get past. "Putting mail into a mailbox should not make me feel this way," Dyrain mumbled to herself as she sat down in one of the lawn chairs. She wondered if she could keep being pen pals with Ien if she had to go through these kinds of troubles every time she mailed off a letter. It was hard enough for her to imagine not being friends with Ien, but to let her parents, whom she thought she was smarter than, find out what she was doing would be a disaster. Dyrain took a deep breath as she scratched her head and looked over her shoulders to see if her mom was near the front room window. She made a quick dash for the mailbox once she saw that the coast was clear. Dyrain was so nervous about her mom seeing her drop mail in the box that she hadn't heard the barks from the neighbor's dog until she walked back to the house. "Oh, be quiet, you little thing." Dyrain stuck her tongue out. Dyrain hoped the next time she sent a letter off would be a lot smoother. A week and a half later, she received a letter and some more of her life story from her pen pal, Ien. She read the pen pal letter first and then the story.

Letter 209

2001/August 21

Dear Dyrain,

It is kind of like knowing the future. The alien race did manipulate peoples' lives the way they wanted it to be. Now that Hysal has documents of almost every human being's life he and his staff of scientists took from the aliens, he is now in control of human life. People think they are living their lives from their own choices and free will, but they are so wrong. Hysal is controlling everything people are doing from how they eat, who they talk to, what they say, and more. People are essentially robots and don't even know it. Hysal basically makes the future. The only thing he can't control is the weather, and he's even working on that. His purpose behind the puppet mastery of human lives is to make it easier to replace the humans once he can find a way to create a new species in his image. Arrogant guy, if you ask me. Once the humans are gone, it would be just a matter of time before he finds my dad and me and the other aliens that escaped. I don't think he would be so kind to just put us away. He would probably experiment on us some more before torching us or feeding us to the wolves. Like I told you before, I convinced my dad that it would not only be rude if I didn't share your own document with you, but it also wouldn't be fair to you since your life is so important to the world. Not only is this the first time an alien is documenting a human's life without any interference since Hysal's grandfather took over, but it's the first time in alien history that an alien is sharing a human's life with the human. Any kind of contact or relationship with you guys is against our law. Sharing a human's life with a human brings the worst punishment an alien can receive. Aliens have to wait until they are fifteen years of age to document a human's life. Even though we document a human's life at an early age, the human can't live it out until they turn twenty-one. I put AWE in capital letters because it's mandatory. AWE is the leader of all aliens. AWE isn't a he or she. AWE is just supreme. One of the things that may be a myth about AWE is that AWE is so powerful that either the word before or after AWE in a sentence has to be in capital letters or something like that. I ignored doing that for your story because, like I said, that might just be a myth. Our supreme alien, AWE, is the author of all human beings' lives until they turn twenty-one, and then we aliens take over. Even though AWE is the author, AWE doesn't control life. So yeah, the first twenty-one years of humans' lives are fully their own. The aliens who got to see AWE seventeen million years ago say AWE sat around all day authoring humans' lives in front of aliens for entertainment until the majority of the aliens rebelled against AWE's wishes and interfered with human lives. Even though AWE still narrates the life of humans to this day, AWE doesn't do it in front of the aliens anymore. Instead of me knowing your every move before you're twenty-one, I have to wait like every other alien 'til you turn twenty-one to know what's going to happen. The alien race is banned from ever seeing or being in the presence of AWE again. That's one awful punishment. AWE is authoring your life right now, and you don't even know it. The alien chosen to document the human's life must be born on the same day and time as the human. That's why I became your pen pal. In some cases, there are more aliens assigned to the same human because they were also born the same day and time as the human. When something like that happens, all the documents on that one human's life are then coordinated into one life document by AWE. I assume it still works like that even with the near destruction of the alien race over a century ago. With our civilization being torn apart, I'm sure that if AWE still exists, AWE would be proud of me for trying to save the alien race. I won't send your whole story from the time you were twenty-one to your death because that's too long. I'll just send you little by little of your life every time we write each other or until my dad thinks it's enough. I really am sorry for controlling your life. I wish I wasn't born this way. It's one of the many gifts I wished AWE hadn't given us aliens. It did nothing but ruin the alien race. Even though my dad and I don't mean any harm to you humans, I can't say that about the rest of my kind. What I can say is that we never tried exterminating the humans, and that should at least count for something. I think it's easier for me to show you in your story why I included Hysal instead of trying to tell you in this letter. It makes it easy for me to write your document in story form when I jot down the dates since you don't want the time on it like I did the original document. I heard the pen that the aliens normally use has a time stamp on it for the timing of every word written down to make it easier to write the human document. I'm sorry I spelled die wrong, but you also have spelled some of your words wrong in your pen pal letters. Actually, I spelled die right; I just put it in the wrong context. Next time, I'll make sure I'll get it right. I didn't know you were an editor because I never claimed to be a Judy Blume, Stephen King, or whomever your favorite author is. Nor am I perfect. AWE is the only perfect alien. I'm satisfied as long as you can understand what I'm trying to say. Even though we aliens have a twelfth sense, and I was only seven years old when I documented your life instead of the required age of fifteen, it's the total opposite when transforming it into a story. You don't understand how hard it is to write it like a story. The few pages in story form I already sent you took me a week to write, and don't forget we aliens don't sleep, so please give me some credit. You couldn't replace the word die because you're a human. Only aliens can make changes on the documents up until that human turns twenty-one and begins to live out the life his or her pen pal created. I figured you would have appreciated me changing your original document because I didn't think that was all that confusing, but oh well. Since I haven't finished changing the rest of the document into story form, I can make the story more simple for you by keeping the "dictionary words" or the sentences that confuse you out of it. Pops is just a nickname. Pops's real name is Ernest. You just haven't read that part of your life where his actual name was mentioned yet. I have to keep those unknown words of people, places, and things in the story because those are actually real words that you and the world will one day use. I'll send you the definition of those words next time I send some of your story, and I will also try to explain the meaning of the words the best I can to you. I personally think the last name Popsic is amazing. Don't be jealous of me because I have a sense of humor and you don't. Without us aliens, you humans would have died off a long time ago from boredom. The things you or any human has ever touched with their hands, have seen with their eyes, and thought of with their minds is from us. Besides the making of you humans, the moon, stars, sky, sun, and the other unbelievable creations, we gave you everything else. Just imagine life without jokes, sports, movies—and that's just a little taste of what we gave you humans. Your ideas, inventions, money, sadness, happiness, and any other thing or place you can think of are from us. The definition of a human being should be an entity who lives with awareness of life he or she thinks is his or hers. I could have made you into a mean parent just like your mom and dad. I could have made your story where you never got married, never had kids, never had any friends. I could have just made you a mean old lady who stayed in a hut all by her lonesome, but I didn't do that to you because I'm not a boring alien.

Your frIENd

"Yeah, I guess you're right, Mom." Kamora tossed her food into her mouth.

"Slow down, honey. Your food can't run from you," Mrs. Popsic told Olina. "You're going to choke on your food."

Mrs. Popsic's words first went into Olina's right ear before they went running out of her left ear. It wasn't that Olina was trying to ignore her mom; she just was so caught up in the wizpire thing that it was hard for her to give even a little attention toward what was going on around her. The way she ate her food had her mom blushing like always when she saw people gobbling her food down in bunches. Mrs. Popsic was wrong this time about somebody eating her food in a hurry because it was delicious. The two girls were trying to eat their way from the table as quickly as possible so they could go get ready for their night out. Olina didn't taste any of the food she ate, because once again, her mind wasn't on anything but going under the moon later that night to see if she was a wizpire. The last time the sisters ate this fast was a couple of years back when they wanted to go to the county fair.

Kamora got up from the table but was stopped by her mom before she could leave the kitchen.

"You know the rules, honey. You have to finish your food if you want some dessert."

"That's all right, Mother. I'll pass on it today."

"It's apple pie with a scoop of ice cream," Mr. Popsic said in a joyful voice.

"I will also pass." Olina joined her sister. Olina slid her plate to the side and slowly backed her wheelchair away from the table.

"You too?" Mrs. Popsic asked. She gave her husband a silent stare down.

He didn't stare back that long because the tasty food stole

his attention back. They sat at the table watching the girls go into their room and close the door.

"I told you those girls are up to something, Sholt."

"Ah, yeah," Sholt agreed with his wife.

"Since when do you know the girls to pass up apple pie with a scoop of ice cream? Since when do you know them to go in their room and close the door?" Mrs. Popsic finished her food. "Sholt, do you hear me?"

"Of course I do, honey."

"Well, aren't they acting kind of weird?"

Mr. Popsic slowly swallowed his food and took a long sip of homemade sweet tea before he answered, "It's all right to have some privacy. We all wanted it as kids." Mr. Popsic burped.

"For me, it was more like shutting my parents out of my life when I was mad at them," Mrs. Popsic said.

"Well, there you go." Mr. Popsic chuckled.

"Oh, hush up, Sholt." Mrs. Popsic frowned.

Back in their room, the girls were going through their preparations step by step. Kamora helped hold her sister up so she could give the second coming speech.

"Come on, Olina. You know you have to hold both your arms up while you talk to the moon."

"I know, but it's hard to hold my arms up because I'm scared I might fall."

"I'm holding you tight. I promise I won't let you fall," Kamora assured her.

Mrs. Popsic knocked on the girls' door but didn't enter. She just wanted to remind the girls to wash up before they went to bed. The knock startled Kamora enough to let Olina slip through her arms. In a coincidence, Mr. Popsic slipped out of his chair at the same time while trying to reach for a napkin across the table.

"What was that noise, Sholt?" Mrs. Popsic looked down the hallway toward the kitchen.

Mr. Popsic ignored his wife. He was too angry to answer her. He quickly jumped up off the floor, wiping the back of his pants and straightening his tie and the work shirt he still wore. He was upset at the napkins for being that far away from him and was mad at the chair for not being tall enough to help him reach the napkins. He wished he could give the napkins and chair a good scolding but knew that would be crazy; instead, he took it out on his wife. "I don't like these chairs in here. You should have bought some better ones!" Mr. Popsic yelled.

"Nobody else complains about the chairs. What's wrong with them, Sholt?"

Mr. Popsic wouldn't dare say the real reason; he didn't want to further shame himself. "None of these chairs are the right color. They're not even comfortable to sit in."

"What are you talking about, Sholt?"

"Never mind, Dyrain. Just never mind." He finished his meal.

Kamora was happy to hear noise from outside her room. Mr. Popsic's fall covered up Olina's fall. It relieved Kamora to know that her parents wouldn't be coming to their door asking questions.

At the moment, Olina didn't care if her parents heard her fall because she was still angry at her big sister for dropping her. Olina was ready to give up on the idea until Kamora convinced her that she would let Olina beat her in every single game on the PlayStation for a whole year if she fell down during her wizpire ceremony. "I can come out the winner either way, because if I am the wizpire, I will be able to beat you in any game we play. I'll be the best in everything." Olina's face lit up like a Christmas tree.

Kamora quickly thought about the deal she made with her sister and how her sister was right if she was indeed a wizpire. "Just remember I could have beaten you a lot worse in all the games we ever played," Kamora said just in case Olina was a wizpire.

The girls went back and forth watching the *Half a Howl* movie and practicing until it was time to go to bed. They whispered, laughed, and talked softly to keep themselves up for another three hours so they could sneak outside. Kamora was the first one to get up when she saw the time was 1:18 a.m. Olina still lay in the bed waiting for her turn to get up.

"What if somebody is up?" Olina asked.

"Shh." Kamora put her finger to her mouth. "That's what I'm checking for," she whispered to Olina as she headed out their room door. It was clear to Kamora that it was going to be an easy exit out of the house once she saw all the lights off in her parents' room through the bottom crack of the door. Kamora was 100 percent sure the coast was clear after pressing her ear against her parents' door. She backed away once she heard snoring coming from the room. She knew her brother had spent the night over at a friend's house, but she still opened his door and turned the light on to see his absence for reassurance. She slowly walked back to her room.

"The coast is clear, little sister. All we need now is the fitted flash and the piece of paper with the words on it."

Olina was excited and all set to go. Once she was in her scholar chair, both girls made their way out of the room. To the girls' surprise, Tugo greeted them at the back door.

"What in heaven's name are you doing up?" Kamora covered her own mouth after talking in her normal voice.

"Mom and Dad will hear you, Kamora," Olina whispered.

Kamora picked Tugo up and took him into the front room.

For some reason, Tugo was defiant and wasn't going to stay put. He ran back toward the girls.

"Tugo wants to come with us," Olina said.

Kamora pointed to the front room and said in a low voice, "Get your tail back in there now, Tugo." Tugo dodged Kamora when she went to grab him for the second time.

"Just let him come, Kamora. He can watch out for us."

"He will wake everyone up with his loud barks. Why are you even up?" Kamora asked the dog and waited for some kind of response.

"When have you known Tugo to ever be a barker?" Olina asked.

"Never, but are you willing to take that chance for this important event?" Kamora asked.

Olina put Tugo on her lap. Kamora went to grab him from her lap but changed her mind after Olina said, "It's all right. He won't make any noise." Kamora put some thought into it for a few seconds, then slowly walked out the back door with Olina following close behind, Tugo still on her lap. The girls looked around the backyard just in case something or somebody was watching. Tugo then jumped from Olina's lap onto the grass. The girls were happy to see the moon cut in half because they would have had to wait until another day for the wizpire ceremony had it been a full moon.

"I've never seen the moon this shiny, ever." Olina smiled at the moon.

"That's because you've never been outside this late to see it." Kamora also smiled at the moon.

Olina thought for a second and said, "We have been outside this late. Do you remember when all of us were coming back from our vacation in Hawaii a long time ago?"

Kamora ignored her sister and instead told her to read the

paper. While Olina went over the movie lines for her ceremony, Kamora watched Tugo run around in circles, chasing his tail.

"I think Tugo prefers the nighttime over the daytime," Kamora said.

Five minutes later, Olina was done rehearsing. "I think I'm all set to go, big sis."

"You think? You have to know, because if you forget what to say, you can't read from the paper again. We won't have another chance. This is our only chance, Olina."

"No, no. I'm sure I'm ready. I've already had a whole day to memorize them." Kamora was hesitant for a few seconds until Olina said, "New life and old life, we separate from doom's night, no more tyrants, done with—" Olina was cut off by her sister.

"All right, I believe you; just save it for the moon." Kamora grabbed the piece of paper from Olina, put it in her pocket, and made way for the ceremony. Kamora had Olina roll after her until she found the best spot in the backyard for Olina to cerminize under the moon. Kamora bear-hugged Olina out of the wheelchair and was able to slowly turn her around to where she could hold Olina up from the back.

"I can barely breathe," Olina struggled to say.

"I'm sorry. I just want to make sure my grip is tight enough to hold you." Kamora loosened her arms just a little bit.

"That's kinda better." Olina sighed a breath of relief.

Both the girls were in position to do their part as they stared up at the moon that shone so brightly.

Olina held her arms up high and recited, "New life and old life / we separate from doom's night / no more tyrants / done with the heathens / mix of blood a scorn of treason / yesterday rise for tomorrow's life / good won't come to know evil's might / lock a wizard in the bing / is hocus-pocus no such thing /

wrath of fire with no belief / ignore blood of vampires' teeth / shoulders of spike / thirsty hikes in plain sight / stay with fear / but run with fear to forget it not / revenge waits to untie knot / hidden princes be of the past / silver gold a turn of brass / freedom howls when wolves growl / fast it comes they all will bow / slow the coming they still will bow / half-moon crown me now." Olina kept her hands raised toward the moon, waiting for her brass crown.

Two minutes passed by without anything happening. "My arms are getting tired, Kamora," Olina moaned.

"Just a little longer; I think I hear your crown coming." Kamora smiled.

Olina begin to hear something also. Kamora continued to hold her sister in a nice, firm grip even though her arms were also tiring. Olina's arms weren't that tired anymore due to excitement running through her body and mind as the noise seemed to get closer and closer. Tugo was also excited, but for different reasons. Tugo turned his attention away from the girls and the moon to focus on some noise by the fence where the garbage was kept.

"It's coming, Kamora! The crown is coming!" Olina yelled in excitement, forgetting that it was one thirty in the morning.

Kamora was too excited herself to tell her sister to keep her voice down. "Yes, I can hear it getting closer," Kamora said, still smiling.

But then reality struck. The noise the sisters heard that they thought was the crown coming was in fact a raccoon digging for garbage. Kamora quickly dropped her sister back into the scholar.

"It's a raccoon," Kamora said with annoyance.

Now looking sad, Olina asked, "Does this mean my crown isn't coming?"

Tugo suddenly raced toward the garbage cans, barking at the raccoon while it sat on top of one of the cans, digging and eating away.

"Tugo, no, no. Tugo, get back here," Kamora whispered urgently.

Tugo's squealing bark seemed to fluster the raccoon, causing it to fall off the garbage can. Kamora had second thoughts about grabbing Tugo once the raccoon was on the ground.

"That thing is huge!" Olina cried out.

Kamora didn't have a choice but to raise her voice in trying to get Tugo's attention. The little dog ignored her and continued to yelp loudly. The girls were more worried about Tugo getting hurt by the raccoon than they were about getting caught outside, until the raccoon suddenly decided to make a run for it. Tugo chased after the raccoon, which was more than twice his size. Olina was frantic in her wheelchair, unsure if she should follow after Kamora, who was now in pursuit of Tugo. The two animals raced through the next-door neighbor's tomato gardens toward a hole in the fence. Kamora could barely keep up. The dark night was making it tough for her to keep Tugo in her sight. Thanks to the raccoon getting stuck in the hole for a few seconds before it made its getaway, Kamora had time to grab Tugo and head back to the house.

Kamora showed amazing willpower and strength while holding Tugo in her left arm and pulling Olina's chair up onto the porch and into the house.

"I could have made it into the house on my own," said Olina.

"I know you could have, but after seeing Mr. Talbert's porch light come on, I couldn't take that chance." Kamora breathed heavily.

"Oh my gosh! He saw us?" Olina asked in a horrified whisper.

"I don't think so," Kamora said uncertainly.

Kamora quietly crept to the front room, where she left Tugo, and then headed toward her room with Olina rolling slowly behind her. The girls felt safe once they were in their room. Exhausted, they really didn't have much to say to each other before going to sleep.

"Good night, Kamora," Olina whispered.

"Good night, Olina, and you don't have to whisper anymore." Kamora pulled the cover over her head and went to sleep.

That following Tuesday morning, June 3, Mr. Popsic was up at his usual time, a quarter to six. Feeling upbeat like every morning, Mr. Popsic hummed his favorite song as he made his way to the kitchen to make his coffee. His humming stopped abruptly when he got to the kitchen.

"What is this?" Mr. Popsic asked aloud, looking at the kitchen floor. He took off his glasses, thinking it would help him have a better view of what he was seeing. Quickly putting his glasses back on, he was now sure of what he saw. He followed the dried-up, muddy tracks toward Kamora and Olina's room door, where they stopped. Mr. Popsic stood in front of the girls' door, wondering how the mud and grass got into the house. A loud knock on the back door interrupted his train of thought. He was able to see some more mud tracks in the front room as he walked toward the back door. He stopped and stared into the front room for a few seconds until he remembered someone was still at the door. "What is this mess?" Mr. Popsic again talked to himself while going to the door. Mr. Popsic open the door after peeping through the curtains. It was Mr. Talbert.

"I'm sorry to bother you this early, Sholt, but I knew this would be a good time to catch you," his neighbor said in a low voice and looked around to make sure his knocking didn't wake anybody else in the house.

"No, it's okay. Come in," Mr. Popsic said, inviting Mr. Talbert inside. Mr. Popsic noticed redness in Mr. Talbert's eyes and dried-up gray lines underneath them as if he'd been crying.

"Yes, um, I wanted to talk to you about my tomato garden being ransacked. I was woken up early this morning by screaming and barking. I looked out my back door, but I didn't see anyone, so I went back to bed. An hour ago, I discovered a footprint in my garden. I'm not saying it was any of your kids, but if you could ask them if they know anything about it, I would appreciate it." Mr. Talbert smiled and nodded before turning to leave.

Mr. Popsic didn't know whether or not he should tell his neighbor about the muddy footprints he'd just discovered. He decided to keep it to himself until he discussed the matter with the girls and his wife. The little man sported a red face. He was livid that one of his kids may have been out in the middle of the night. He was so close to waking the whole house, but knew doing so would make him late to work and decided against it. It usually took him thirty minutes for his morning routine before leaving for work. This time, it took him close to forty-five minutes, and he still forgot the lunch his wife packed for him the day before. A note Mr. Popsic wrote before he left played a part in his late departure. The note was taped to the back of a chair that blocked the hallway. "Can't miss it," Mr. Popsic mumbled to himself as he sat the chair in the middle of the hallway.

Mrs. Popsic was the first one to read the note that morning:

> *If you girls read this note before your mom, you'd better make sure she reads it after you, or I promise you it will be double the trouble when I get back from work. You girls are in big trouble. You have some explaining to do for the house looking like a zoo. And*

don't you try to rehearse lies with your sister, Kamora, because it won't work. Nobody is allowed to play any games, and you're only allowed to go outside when your mother takes you girls with her to drop Sammy off at the airport. Dyrain, honey, make sure the first thing they do when they get up is clean up. Don't let them eat, brush their teeth, wash up, or anything. Cleaning is what they will do before anything else. I will be back!!!

Mrs. Popsic was baffled so much by the note that she read it again. After reading it a second time, she finally looked at the hallway floor to see the dried-up mud tracks her husband was talking about. She followed the tracks into the kitchen, taking the chair with her. "Oh my," Mrs. Popsic said, covering her mouth with both hands. She slowly turned in a circle to get a full view of the floor. Mrs. Popsic aggressively put her hands on her hips and asked aloud, "Who would do something like this?" Mrs. Popsic started to fetch the steam cleaner until she remembered Kamora had accidently broken it a few weeks earlier. She wasn't going to let that stop her from her cleaning. She was thirty-five minutes into the cleaning when Sammy arrived home from his friend's house.

"We have about a couple of hours until my plane leaves," Sammy reminded his mom after pouring himself a cup of Kool-Aid. "What's that you're cleaning, Mom?" Sammy watched his mom scrub the last of the dirt from the carpet in the front room.

"Just some dirt," she answered back.

Sammy wondered why his mom needed such a big bucket of water for such a small cleaning, but didn't bother asking her about it.

"Where are the girls?" Sammy asked.

"I think they're still asleep," Mrs. Popsic said.

"Sleep? It's almost eleven thirty. What are they still doing asleep?" Sammy asked as he walked to his room.

Mrs. Popsic was so caught up in cleaning that she didn't realize how late the girls were sleeping. "Wake them up for me, honey!" she bellowed. She just then noticed the dirt on Tugo when she scooted his basket out of the way while he slept. She picked up the sleeping dog to get a better look. "Ooh, you need a cleaning, and you smell. What have you been in?" Mrs. Popsic asked. She took Tugo downstairs and put him in the doggyshire for a good fifteen minutes.

The girls were at the table eating cereal when Mrs. Popsic came back upstairs with Tugo. They had no idea of the overwhelming evidence they had left behind for their parents to see.

"Did you guys read the note your father wrote yet?" Mrs. Popsic pointed at the piece of paper on the table.

The girls didn't have the slightest clue what their mom was talking about. Kamora casually reached for the paper, picked it up, and read it. She suddenly dropped her spoon in her cereal bowl, causing some of the milk to splash onto the note. Kamora looked at her mom and then gave Olina a worried kind of stare.

"What does it say, Kamora?" Olina gave Kamora a worried stare back.

Kamora's eyes quickly landed back on her mom, watching her clean Tugo's sleeping basket. Kamora didn't know how to respond to the note. She had no words. She wasn't prepared to answer her mom like she normally would be when she did something wrong. Olina continued to eat her cereal, still unaware of what was on the note.

"What does it say?" Olina asked again.

Kamora tried whispering to Olina what the note said while Mrs. Popsic had her back turned as she continued cleaning. Olina frowned because she couldn't hear and was confused as to why Kamora was whispering.

"What?" Olina blurted.

Mrs. Popsic turned back toward the girls and said, "Well, what happened?"

Kamora went into dumb mode. "Why would Dad write a crazy note like this?" Kamora smiled nervously. She couldn't believe she'd tracked mud through the house without realizing it.

"That's what I'm trying to figure out. It was dried-up mud tracks and grass throughout the house that I had to clean," said Mrs. Popsic.

Kamora said nothing. Olina was still kind of slow to catch on to what the note or her mom was talking about, so she also kept silent.

"Tugo had dirt all over him and his sleeping basket. I just got through cleaning him up in the doggyshire," Mrs. Popsic continued.

"How did Tugo make all that mess?" Kamora asked, trying to pass the blame.

Mrs. Popsic smiled at her daughter and said, "You must have forgotten about the footprints I said I also cleaned up that looked"—Mrs. Popsic paused and looked down at Kamora's feet—"about your size."

Olina was frustrated that she still didn't know what was going on. She tried grabbing the note from Kamora to read it but had a hard time reaching across the table. "Let me read the note, Kamora. What does it say?" Olina asked.

Kamora's brain was racing to think up more ways to throw her mom off track but found it hard with Olina badgering her.

"Kamora, what is on the note?" Olina asked once again.

"It's about last night!" Kamora shrieked at her sister. She instantly regretted the outburst.

Mrs. Popsic put her hands on her hips. "Yeah, well, you explain last night to your father when he gets back from work, and hurry up with breakfast so we can take Sammy to the airport." She then walked to her room.

Kamora was angry and done with her breakfast. "You see what you did." Kamora scowled at her sister.

"What did I do?" Olina still really didn't know what was going on.

"Are you stupid or what, Olina? Mom was talking about what we did last night. The wizpire, the moon, the ceremony, the raccoon, the loudmouth Tugo. Do you want me to spell it out for you? No, better yet, I can try putting us on the eqi so you can know what I'm talking about."

"I'm sorry. I didn't know what you were talking about," Olina said, her feelings hurt.

"It's too late for sorry. Mom knows it was us now because I gave it away. You made me give it away. I don't know what lie I can think up to tell Dad now." Kamora looked around the kitchen in despair.

An hour and a half later, the Popsic family made it to the airport to drop off Sammy. Mrs. Popsic, along with the girls, went inside the airport with Sammy.

"Wow! This place is big," Olina said, looking up at the ceiling.

"Yeah, it is." Sammy looked back at Olina as he carried his two suitcases.

"Will those be enough clothes to last you?" Mrs. Popsic asked.

"Oh yeah. Summer school is only for a couple of months, and I'm only attending class twice a week," Sammy answered.

"Okay, well, if you do get down there and you need

anything from the house, just call me and I'll contact Traveler's Circle," Mrs. Popsic reminded him.

The girls slowed up to look at one of the many pieces being built for the zoomeda.

"Mom and Sammy, come look at one of the doors being built for the zoomeda!" Olina was excited.

The metal door was being worked on by close to fifty workers as other bystanders watched with excitement. Kamora held on to Olina's chair.

"Stop it, Kamora." Olina frowned.

"Mom, Olina is trying to pass the sign," Kamora tattled on her sister.

"We have to stay behind the sign so we don't interfere with the workers." Mrs. Popsic rubbed Olina's head.

"It would be lovely if the zoomeda was done today." Sammy smiled and looked on in amazement.

"Another twenty-one months until it's finished," Kamora noted as she looked at the countdown displayed in the glass above the working zone.

"Why is it taking so long to finish?" Olina looked up at her mom for an answer.

A twelve-year-old boy in the crowd standing next to Olina said, "My dad tells me they will never finish such a project because the zoomeda is a scam. Right, Dad?" The boy looked at his dad.

"How is it a scam?" Kamora frowned.

"My dad says this is just another way of getting money from us taxpayers," the boy finished.

"That doesn't mean it's a scam," Kamora looked at the boy's father.

"It would only be a scam if they weren't working on anything." Mrs. Popsic also looked at the boy's father.

"Don't matter if they're working on it. The zoomeda is a scam because it's not going to work," the man huffed. "I don't see how some machine is going to be able to get people from here to Russia, Germany, or to any other place in five or ten minutes. It's just impossible." The angry man grabbed his son by the hand and stomped off.

Mrs. Popsic called after him, "Yeah, they also said the airplane was impossible."

The intercom announced Sammy's plane departure. Mrs. Popsic and the girls gave Sammy hugs and kisses before he entered the bodtic.

"You're going to make me miss my plane," Sammy joked with Olina while she hugged him tightly.

The three stood behind the gates, watching Sammy go through the bodtic and out toward his plane.

"Remember to call when you make it there!" Mrs. Popsic reminded her son for the fourth time.

Sammy nodded before he was finally out of their sight.

A few hours later back on Glencoe Drive, Mrs. Popsic was setting the table for dinner. Kamora talked on the phone while Olina played on the computer. The day seemed like it was going to finish out pleasantly—until Mr. Popsic walked through the front door.

Instead of his usual "hi" to the girls and his wife, he planted his eyes directly on the carpet. He made his way to the hallway and then to the kitchen. Mr. Popsic was pleased to see the floors cleaned. He slowly untied his tie as he said, "You girls did a good job. The floors look much better than this morning."

"You mean *I* did a good job," Mrs. Popsic said, surprising her husband.

Mr. Popsic stopped fooling with his tie to put his hands on his hips. Not able to talk right away because he was angry, he stared at his wife for a few seconds. He'd known it was a possibility that she would have cleaned up for the girls, but he hadn't thought he would have to tell his wife not to, since he thought the note would convince her of just how mad he was. Mr. Popsic did a good job of holding his temper as he calmly asked his wife to join him in their bedroom so they could talk privately.

Kamora ended her phone call after she heard a commotion coming from their parents' room, and she headed down the hallway to see what the fuss was about, Olina following her. Kamora squatted down, pressing her ear against the door for a better listen.

"What are they saying?" Olina whispered.

Kamora held her finger up toward Olina, signaling her to hold on. Kamora, unaware of her parents' room door not being shut tightly, accidently opened the door while trying to listen and fell forward into the room, giving her parents a perfect view of her.

"Reverse right now!" Olina yelled at her scholar.

"Don't worry, girls. You will get your turn," Mr. Popsic said in a deep voice. Mrs. Popsic hurried to the door and closed it so they could finish their conversation.

"I never heard Dad sound like that," said Olina.

"I've never seen his face that red," Kamora said.

Mr. Popsic took a peek out of the door after his wife shut it to see if the girls would dare try to be nosy again.

"Oh, stop it, Sholt. Close the door." Mrs. Popsic frowned.

"So, like I was saying, the only solution I can ... I *will* accept is for them to be grounded for at least a month or until I say it's over." Mr. Popsic's voice was aggressive. He didn't agree with his wife's facial expression as she started to talk, so he instead talked over her, showing her he meant business. "Nope, I don't want to hear it, Dyrain. This is an executive decision coming down from the man of the house. It's my way or no way, and I don't care if you look at me with your face all twisted up. This is the way it's going to be," Mr. Popsic finished saying.

Some of his words, as well as his body language, sounded all too familiar to his wife. It didn't take Mrs. Popsic long to figure out her husband was not only reciting words from the book *Firm Action*, but he at the same time was emulating the quirky body movements of Vice President Lora Ramirez. She didn't waste any time exposing her husband. She even fetched the book *Firm Action* from the closet, where he thought it was safely hidden in his shoe box.

His stomach sank to the floor when he saw her grab the book. He felt a mix of emotions going through his body. Too angry to think straight and too embarrassed to try defending himself, Mr. Popsic grabbed a towel off his bed and threw it near his wife's feet before sitting down. "I give up. I throw in the towel. You always win," Mr. Popsic said, displaying a discomforting smile.

His wife of twenty-two years sat down next to him on the bed. She took his glasses off so she could give him a good long kiss on the lips.

"Why'd you do that?" Mr. Popsic looked surprised. "Aren't you mad at me?"

Mrs. Popsic smiled and said, "I'm mad at William Hanson for writing this book." She held the book up and tossed it into the garbage can.

Mr. Popsic's body jerked quickly toward the garbage can to retrieve his book, but he changed his mind and continued sitting on the bed, listening to his wife.

"It tickles me to see you copy the vice president. It's funny how twenty or thirty years ago a man would have been ridiculed for mimicking a female. Oh, how times have changed." Mrs. Popsic patted her husband's leg, and his demeanor began to soften as she spoke. "I'd like to see you try using that method at work on your boss. You don't have to be King Kong to get your point across, Sholt. Huffing and puffing like the Big Bad Wolf is not you. Being intelligent, smart, charismatic, nerdy, and loveable are some of the good things that make *you*. Those are the qualities that made me fall in love with you and that keep me in love with you today. This is not a communist marriage, and you're not a dictator. Why do you think William Hanson's wife divorced him?" Mr. and Mrs. Popsic both laughed. Mrs. Popsic continued to scold her husband, but it was in a way that made him appreciate himself. "We decided to get married in the year 2009, April 7. That's when we became one … *uno*. No more individual self. We are a married couple, a team." Mrs. Popsic broke down a little bit of what marriage is supposed to be about.

"Give it to me; I deserve it," Mr. Popsic playfully encouraged the chastising.

"I agree with you that the girls need to be punished, and a punishment they will get. That punishment will be handed down from both the parents," Mrs. Popsic said with confidence.

After coming to an agreement, Mr. and Mrs. Popsic were ready to talk to the girls. Kamora didn't waste any time telling her parents the truth from beginning to end since lying was pointless, as her parents already knew too much about last night.

"That's what happens when you go snooping around being nosy," Mrs. Popsic said as she finished setting the table.

"Now you guys should know better than to think that your mom or I would think you girls would be some half-wolf character," Mr. Popsic said.

"No, Dad, the wizpire is a half wizard and half vampire that's in the *Half a Howl* movie for—" Olina's sentence was interrupted by her dad.

"Yeah, all right. I understand, darling," Mr. Popsic said as he sat down at the table.

Mr. and Mrs. Popsic spent twenty minutes eating and explaining the girls' punishment to them. Kamora and Olina could hardly eat.

"Yesterday, I barely ate because of excitement. Today, I'm having a hard time eating because I'm upset. I wonder what tomorrow will bring," Kamora stated as she stared at her food.

"Hopefully, you girls will learn from this." Mrs. Popsic smiled.

"You girls should be praising your mother because, without her, you girls would not be going to the mall next week." Mr. Popsic took a break from his food.

"We weren't going to get to see SkijFris?" Olina's forehead went up in wrinkles.

Kamora was also surprised like Olina, staring at her dad with her mouth open and her chin hanging. "Are you serious, Dad?" Kamora asked.

Mr. Popsic put a spoonful of macaroni in his mouth and nodded. The punishment they received didn't seem all that bad after hearing they almost missed seeing their idol.

The girls had to wait a few days until Friday, June 6, to work on fixing Mr. Talbert's tomato garden. Mr. Talbert was all smiles when he showed up at the Popsics' to let them know the new garden tools he'd ordered days ago had finally arrived. The girls weren't all smiles when their neighbor showed up.

"And don't forget to apologize to him," Mrs. Popsic whispered sternly before sending the girls outdoors.

The two followed Mr. Talbert to his house.

"I don't think it will be all that bad, Kamora," Olina said.

Kamora was motivated by her younger sister's positive attitude. "Yeah, right? What can be so hard about putting tomatoes in the grass."

The girls smiled at each other. Mr. Talbert listened to the girls and was amused by what they thought it took to make a tomato garden.

"I'm sorry for running in your garden, Mr. Talbert." Kamora looked at the back of the sixty-three-year-old man's head as he walked.

"Have you girls ever made a tomato garden or any other kind of garden?" he asked, smiling at them. He wanted to hear more of their amusing youthful thinking.

"I made a tulip garden a long time ago," Olina said happily.

Kamora wanted to tell her sister that she couldn't make a garden out of tulips, but wasn't sure of herself and waited to hear what the old man had to say. Mr. Talbert didn't respond to Olina's statement with words. He instead turned to Olina and smiled. Kamora took the smile as a yes and was upset and amazed that her younger sister knew something she didn't know.

Are you freaking kidding me? I didn't know a person could make a garden out of tulips, Kamora thought. That was one of the many times Kamora was stunned to know Olina knew something she didn't know.

"How about you?" The gray-haired man turned to Kamora.

Kamora didn't want to be outdone by her younger sister or give her any kind of clue that she was smarter about something. Kamora thought for a second and said, "I just remember helping Olina with her garden. I would pour water on it and stuff and other things when needed because, of course, I wanted the garden to last," Kamora answered.

Olina didn't remember her sister doing anything to help with her tulip garden, and she looked up at Kamora with confusion on her face. Kamora recognized the look of confusion.

"I did those things when you weren't around." Kamora smiled at her sister.

Mr. Talbert grabbed the hoe from his shed when they got to his backyard. He gave both the girls bandannas to wrap around their heads.

"You can be on standby," Mr. Talbert told Olina. "Just sit back until I have something for you to do, since you weren't the one who ruined my precious tomatoes." After giving Kamora the hoe, he pulled back the black plastic from over the garden. This was the first time he'd seen the ruined garden since the morning of the incident. Mr. Talbert put his hands up toward his mouth and said, "This is worse than I thought it was."

The girls watched his face vibrate like a volcano before its eruption. After seeing their father in angry mode over the years, they knew what was coming next. They braced themselves for the loud screaming Mr. Talbert was about to unleash on them. Kamora was the first to plug her ears with her fingers, with Olina following suit. The girls were right to prepare themselves for a meltdown, but it wasn't the kind they were expecting. A whimpering sound a puppy or a kitten would make when hungry escaped the old man's mouth. Olina and Kamora both wore frowns on their faces when they looked at each other. They slowly pulled their fingers from their ears and then turned to him, waiting for the punch line. The girls stared at Mr. Talbert in silence, trying to understand what he was doing.

"Okay," Kamora said softly, trying getting Mr. Talbert's attention.

"I think he really is crying," Olina said as she rolled closer to him.

A lady the girls thought was Mr. Talbert's daughter came out of the house. She swiped the handkerchief from Mr. Talbert's back pocket to dry his tears. The girls were more puzzled than ever.

"Kamora already told him she was sorry for running in his garden," Olina said, looking at the lady.

"No, don't cry. It's all right. You're all right. It won't look like this in a couple of hours, I promise." The lady consoled Mr. Talbert like he was her baby before turning to the girls. "Oh, don't worry, girls. Drew sometimes gets emotional when it comes to his garden." She continued to console him.

Kamora's face turned sour when she saw how the woman was cheering up Mr. Talbert. She was shocked to see her kiss Mr. Talbert on the lips and massage his neck like he was her husband and not the daughter they thought she was. It seemed to get the job done because Mr. Talbert was back to normal in a matter of minutes.

"Holler for me if you need me, Drew," she said as she walked back to the house after Mr. Talbert smiled and winked at her.

He quickly turned his attention to Kamora. "The first thing you're going to do is prepare the soil by tilling it ten inches."

"Till what inches?" Kamora tucked the rest of her hair underneath the bandanna.

Mr. Talbert grabbed the hoe away from Kamora to demonstrate the tilling process. Then he went to the next step. "This is exactly how you're going to do the second part," Mr. Talbert stated as he broke up soil clumps.

"I have to do all this for a tomato garden?" Kamora's face sank.

"You didn't think it was going to be a walk in the park, did you? Or a run in my tomato garden?" He burst out in laughter.

Either the girls didn't get the joke or they didn't care enough to laugh. Mr. Talbert continued laughing despite getting weird looks from the girls.

Angry that the woman in Mr. Talbert's house wasn't going to help out with the tomato garden, and wanting to know for sure if she was his daughter or not, Kamora decided to kill two birds with one stone. "Is your daughter going to help us with the garden?"

Mr. Talbert immediately stopped laughing and said, "First and foremost, she's not my daughter, and she's not going to help you. She's not the one who smashed my cages, kicked up my dirt, or put footprints all over my dang garden." Mr. Talbert looked at Kamora while pointing at the garden. Kamora was surprised at what Mr. Talbert said.

"You said a bad word!" Olina covered her mouth with one hand and pointed at Mr. Talbert with the other one.

Mr. Talbert ignored the girl's reaction and demonstrated the third step in preparing the tomato garden. "Okay, after breaking up the soil clumps and removing the rocks and sticks, you're going to add three inches of compost to the soil and turn it in so it mixes with the top six inches of soil." Mr. Talbert worked as he spoke. He explained and demonstrated for several more minutes. "The last thing to do is to put the tomato cages around the garden," he finished. Kamora stood still until Mr. Talbert said, "Standing still won't get you out of your punishment. The quicker you start, the better." Mr. Talbert wiped his brow.

Kamora rolled her eyes at her elder and began to work. Kamora did nearly all the work by herself, with Olina helping out every now and then when Kamora needed a cup of water or a tool passed to her. Mr. Talbert would guide Kamora and repeat the instructions to her over and over again until she would complete whatever step she was working on. After about twenty minutes, Kamora stopped digging and lay on her back to rest.

"You're almost done," said Mr. Talbert. "All you have to do now is plant the seeds, cover the holes, and, of course, put up the tomato cages," he stood over Kamora, unintentionally blocking the sun from her view.

"Thanks for keeping the sun out of my face." Kamora smiled at Mr. Talbert.

"You're mean," Olina said to Mr. Talbert after watching him quickly scoot out of the sun's way. Olina tried blocking the sun for her sister, but she was too short. "I'd be able to block it for you if I wasn't in this stupid wheelchair," Olina said, frustrated.

"Don't worry, little sis. You can get me some water instead." Kamora slowly sat up.

Mr. Talbert stood staring at Kamora with his fists balled up on his hips. "You rested almost five minutes already. Let's go. It's dang near close to my dinnertime," Mr. Talbert frowned.

"Ooh! You said a bad word again." Olina's eyes grew big.

"*Dang* isn't a curse word," he barked at Olina.

"Let's get going, girl." He stretched his neck out toward Kamora with his hands still on his hips.

"I'm going to tell my mom and dad you're mean!" Olina yelled.

"I'm going to tell my mom and dad you're mean!" Mr. Talbert mockingly danced around in a circle while repeating Olina's threat.

Anger immediately gripped Kamora. She began to think about how she had gotten into this situation in the first place. Her mind raced. She was mad that she had thought Olina was a wizpire, mad at herself for letting Tugo come outside with them, and mad that she tracked mud in the house, but most of all she was mad at how Mr. Talbert was treating her and Olina. She wanted to walk away without finishing the job, and if she didn't think she would get punished again, she would have quit, because at this point, she really didn't care whether or not she saw SkijFris. Kamora inhaled deeply, blew out a breath of hot air, and went back to work furiously, fueled by her anger. Kamora refused a second cup of water from her sister because she thought it would knock her mind out of the zone it had entered. Olina sat in her chair with a nervous look on her face as she watched her sister work. Olina had never seen her sister move so fast before.

"You positive you don't need any water, Kamora?" Olina tried passing her sister the cup of water again a little while later.

Kamora smacked the cup from her sister's hand, splashing the water on Mr. Talbert's clothes.

"What the heck!" Mr. Talbert yelled.

"Ooh." Olina pointed, surprised at her sister's action.

"Shut up!" Mr. Talbert snapped.

The young lady came back outside upon hearing his yells to see what was going on.

"All done. It looks like Olina and I will be leaving," Kamora jumped for joy.

"Look, Kamora! He used the bathroom on himself!" Olina pointed and laughed.

The young lady thought to be Mr. Talbert's daughter yanked the handkerchief from his back pocket and begin to pat dry the water that had splashed onto his pants.

"Hey, I'm not done with you guys. Come back here and put the tools in the shed," Mr. Talbert commanded, trying to think of anything to make them suffer longer.

Kamora did as she was told as quickly as possible before

turning to head home. "You don't ever have to worry about me being in your stupid garden again," Kamora said as she walked off.

"Yeah, me neither." Olina rolled behind Kamora.

The girls were relieved to be home and out of that nightmare. Kamora was the first one through the back door. "We finally made it back!" Kamora called as she walked toward the front room.

Mrs. Popsic hushed Kamora with her finger.

"Oh, company," Kamora whispered apologetically after seeing her parents in the front room with two businesswomen. She headed down the hall to her room.

"Mom and Dad, you guys won't believe what happened to us!" Olina had just made it into the house.

"We will talk about it later, honey." Mrs. Popsic smiled at Olina, gesturing to her that they had company.

Mrs. Popsic was having a hard time choosing between two businesses interested in selling the garments she sewed. "If I could choose both of your stores to sell my product, God knows I would, but, of course, that's not an option because of the contract disputes." Mrs. Popsic turned to her husband and smiled. "What should I do, Sholt?"

"I'm going to leave this up to the experts," Mr. Popsic said. He kept quiet and continued to listen to his wife converse with the two business associates.

Letter 210

2001/October 2

Dear Ien,

What is up with my pen pal? I know I took a while to write back. I'll be honest with you, I started reading the story about two weeks after you sent it to me, and I just finished about a week ago. I wish I didn't have so much homework to do because I could have read the story already. Of course, I know I don't have to explain myself because I know you already understand. I thought the freshman teachers were hard on us last year with the homework, but I would have to say I am getting even more homework this year. If it is like this my junior year, I'm going to have to ditch school for good. I also had to hold off from writing this letter for a few days because I had to rehearse my lines for the stupid choir class. I tried dropping my choir class because I don't want to fly to another country just to perform. I tried explaining to my teacher that I was scared to get on a plane after what happen to Aaliyah and the World Trade Center. All she would tell me is that choir class is mandatory for graduating. She couldn't care less about my feelings. I hate her and school. But anyway, I have a million and one things I want to say to you, Mr. Ien. First, I'd like to tell you that I won't ask you to change my story again because I'm sure I'm always going to find something I don't like in the story and probably would keep telling you to change it. Thanks for keeping those big words and those confusing sentences out of the story. The story is much easier for me to read. I also want to tell you that you are one tricky individual. I did some research on your story and found some of the important things to be accurate, like the dates for the future. That's only because you used Google to find the information you need. Even though it seems like you have all your bases covered, I found some things in the story that don't make sense to me. I said to myself that I'm going to pretend that your documentation on my life is true and thought of some questions

I wanted to ask. It took me a couple of days to think of them all. I numbered my questions to make it easy for you to answer them:

0) How can you guys make the future without controlling the weather?

1) You say you're not from mysterious planets, so where are you and the rest of the aliens from?

2) What happens when an alien documents a human's life and that human dies before he or she is twenty-one?

3) When a human being dies young, say like at twenty-five, whose fault is that—and if it is an alien's fault, then why didn't the alien stop the human's death since the alien is in control?

4) You say you aliens didn't look like ET, so what did you guys look like?

5) If you guys have or had so much control over us humans, then how was Hysal's grandfather able to take control over you aliens?

6) Do you have your own language?

7) You say this is the documentation of my life, but it seems more like a documentation on Kamora's and Olina's lives because you talk about them more. Why?

8) Why would you make my daughter handicapped?

9) Why didn't you give my character a better talent than sewing?

10) If you're just in charge of my life, then how do you know what the other people in the story will say or do in the future?

11) If you are who you say you are, can you prove it to me? The stuff you tell me about the future and the past proves nothing.

12) If I weren't born, would Kamora and Olina be born? Who would Sholt be married to, and where would Sammy be?

13) How old do you guys get to live to since you never die?

14) Are there any female aliens?

15) Once I turn twenty-one and start living out the life you penned out for me, will I remember you and this pen pal stuff?

16) I don't think it's fair for kids at your school to see what you look like and I can't.

17) Who are my children's pen pals?

If I didn't have so much homework, I could have thought of at least a hundred more things to ask you. Well, that's all I have to say for right now. Oh yeah, I almost forgot to tell you to just send me about ten to fifteen pages of the story next time. Once I get this homework out of the way, you can send me more. Write me back right away.

Your friend, Dyrain

Letter 211

2001/ October 11

Dear Dyrain,

You should be the last one to say that you hate teachers. You act just like one sometimes, especially when you try giving me editing advice. If I ever do change your story again, I promise I will make you a schoolteacher instead of a homeschool one. The majority of the questions you ask are what my dad and I hope to find out through your story one day. I never said we completely make the future. Yes, there are female aliens. As far as I know, you will not remember anything about me or our friendship once you turn twenty-one. Was number sixteen a question? You are right about the students seeing me, but if they knew I was an alien, I guarantee my dad would have never let them see me. You are the only person who knows what I am, and, therefore, like I told you before, it would be too risky for you to ever see me. This is a documentation of your life, not Kamora's or Olina's, but they are part of your life just like the mailman who delivers your mail. Every person, place, and thing plays a role in your life and can't be left out the story whether it's talked about more or less. Olina being handicapped is not as bad as you think it is. She can do everything other kids can do except for walk, and that still doesn't stop her from getting around. Are you jealous that she is more special than you? A mom jealous of her own daughter? What a shame. I knew you would soon ask me about your sewing talent. The human inherits the gift of the alien who documents his or her life. The human is something like a "chip off the old block." The human has the same personality as the alien who documents his or her life. That's why you have mad people, nice people, evil, angry, and other different characteristics of the human race. Your gift of sewing came from me. I didn't want to tell you that one because I was ashamed for you to know that I can sew, but I choose not to sew because that's a girly thing. AWE gives every alien many gifts, and that's the one you inherited from me. I'll send you only about ten pages of your story because I do understand how busy you are. I'll also send you the dictionary of future words I said I would send you, and I'll try explaining them to you as best I can.

Your frIENd

Letter 212

2001/October 16

Dear Ien,

The mailman and my daughters are equally part of my life? How can you even compare the mailman to Kamora and Olina? Why would I be jealous of my own daughter? If I am jealous of my own daughter, that makes you the stupid one because you made it that way. Sewing is not a girly thing. I can't believe you blew the rest of my questions off as a joke. You say you and your dad respect me more for me reading this so-called story of mine, but you sure don't act like it. Do you know what I go through just to receive your letters? Do you have any idea of the struggle I go through just to write you or send letters back to you? How do you think I feel having a friend for five years who I've never seen before or who I can't talk to on the phone because he, she, it, or whatever you are continues trying to manipulate me into thinking you're something from another planet? The word foreign *should be spelled* forIen *because that best describes your character. Everything you're doing is for Ien and nobody else. You are selfish. You are right about being an alien, just not the kind of one you claim to be. You're a creepy stranger instead of a pen pal. That trick you did with the document so I can't write on it or change anything didn't convince me to believe your story. You're just a sick human taking advantage of a "naïve" teenager. You say it's impossible for you to answer my questions, but you're the one who said, I quote, "Just imagine life without jokes, sports, movies—and that's just a little taste of what we gave you humans." How can you give us humans such great things, but you can't give a teenage girl simple answers? I knew I should have stopped this pen pal stuff. I find it hard to stop writing and reading your letters the more time I invest in this "friendship."*

The main reason I haven't stopped writing you is because I don't have that many friends and I am bored. I feel totally stupid every time I write you or read your letters. This is really beginning to be too much for me.

Dyrain

Letter 213

2001/October 21

Dear Dyrain,

I think that's rude to say that I'm a stranger and not your pen pal. I knew you were mad when your letter came so fast. I'm not controlling your life right now, so you being jealous of Olina at this point in your life has nothing to do with me. I guess you would be able to quote everything I ever wrote to you and even though I don't remember saying that, I do stick by it because it's true. I didn't mean it in the way you thought I did when I talked about the mailman and the girls. I would never compare a stranger to your loved ones. You took it the wrong way when you asked me why I talk about the girls more than you in the story, and I said they are part of your life like the mailman is. I should have told you it was because I changed the document into story form. An author's novel and an alien's document can tell the same story, but it will be in a different way. If I would have kept it in document form, not only would you be the main character, but it's mandatory to include you in every part of it because it's alien law. The main character in a novel doesn't have to be included in every part of the story, and unlike in your document, anybody can be a main character. It's impossible for a normal human being to save the alien or human race. It takes a special kind of human. In your story, I decided to make Olina, who is handicapped, the main character for the purpose of defeating Hysal, and, of course, we won't know for sure if it will work until that certain part of your life is actually lived out. I know that's a long time for answers, but what other options do I have? You're right about me not having control over the other people's lives in the story, but that doesn't mean I can't make them part of the story because when it's all said and done, AWE will organize your life and everyone in your life the way he wants it. I know I sound all over the place with everything I'm talking about. I understand why you don't believe me being an alien. I also wouldn't believe it if I were a human and somebody was telling me he or she was an alien. I'm dead serious about who I am, and yes, it is tough for me to prove that right now because, like I told you before, I'm clueless about the majority of alien history. Some of the things I do know were passed down from the older aliens who were held in captivity with me and my dad. I could have learned more if I had more time to talk to the older aliens. The only time Hysal left us alone is when it was bedtime for him and his workers. Since we aliens never sleep, that was our only free time with each other. We would talk nonstop with each other about everything and anything we thought of that could help us preserve our history while we plotted our escape. That's where I first gained a part of the history of my aliencestry. Most of our knowledge about our alien past came from a notebook we stole when we escaped. That notebook has a bunch of information that was dated from the time Vrokma found us. I would assume the notebook was passed all the way down to Hysal, and now we have it. If it were up to me, I would send it to you, but my dad says it would be too dangerous and a waste of time for you to look at. Our age process is complicated, just like everything else since Vrokma found us. We don't have any information on what we looked like before we conformed to look like you humans. The only thing jotted down in the notebook about our looks is that our looks were "of a familiar scent." I could have known what that meant if there were more information in the notebook about our looks. I don't remember telling you we weren't from another planet. I don't know where we came from. That's one of the questions I want to have answered myself. As far as I know, aliens live forever, but since we now look like humans, our aging stops at sixty years of age. So even if we're millions of years old, the oldest we would look is like a sixty-year-old person. When a human dies at a young age over twenty-one, it is the alien's fault because the alien is in control of that human's life. There are a lot of reasons why the alien might make the human die young. I heard it didn't used to be like that until the aliens were punished for rebelling against AWE. Olina has a pen pal just like every other human, and no, I don't know who it is, but that won't interfere with your story because I'm sure Olina's pen pal is one of the aliens who had his or her mind intercepted by Hysal already. I promise those are the only questions I can answer for you. The other questions you want to know are impossible for me to answer because I don't know them myself. I'm so afraid of you not wanting to be my friend that I was going to make up answers just to satisfy you, but my dad wouldn't let me. Please don't be mad at me, Dyrain. I will never ignore your questions on purpose. From here on out, even if I don't have the answers to them, I will at least explain to you why I can't answer them. I love you, and I hope to hear from you soon. My dad also wrote you a letter, which is enclosed with this one.

Still your friend, Ien

How are you doing, Dyrain? This is Cortez. The first thing I must do is apologize for my son saying it's a girly thing to sew. He has better manners than that. I would have erased that part if I didn't forget to read over that letter. Last time I wrote you was almost three years ago when you and Ien weren't on speaking terms. I hope this isn't that same situation where I have to remind the two of you that it's all right for friends to get mad at each other, but not stay mad at each other. It's my duty to step in when you're feeling like you're not being appreciated. Both my son and I were overjoyed the first time you read your original document, and we feel that same way today. We respect the fact that you may not believe we are who we say we are. That's why I'm still surprised you continue to read my son's letters and write back to him. Your friendship isn't needed to help our cause, but it's wanted, and that's just as important. You keep our minds in good health. It does hurt to have you not believe we are aliens, but it still gives us a good feeling to be able to admit our true selves to you. You make us outsiders feel like family, and that's something my son and I have never felt from another human who knew we were aliens, or, in your case, strangers. Believe me when I tell you that I understand your struggle to receive and read letters from my son and to write and send him letters in return. It's because of you that I did research on the teenage girl to understand you better. I heard about your editing skills, so please don't take my researching the teenage girl out of context. I know being a teenager is tough in so many ways. Parents not listening to what you have to say, trying to finish weekend homework just so you can be allowed to attend homecoming, boyfriend trouble, girlfriend trouble, too many chores, not enough allowance, early curfew, and on top of all that, you put up with me and my son. You are truly a special young lady. I have seen positive changes in my son since you and he became friends. I don't think he knew what a mailbox was until you two started sending each other letters. Nowadays, Ien checks for your letters before the mailman arrives. Before you two sent each other mail, I remember when I would have to remind Ien over and over to get the mail just to end up still bringing the mail in myself.

You help bring out the best in my son. The kid is hard at work for his alien nation. You should have seen him those first few weeks when he began to transform your original document into story form. Ien would race home every day with new novels to read to broaden his writing skills. Besides the helpful books you sent him, Ien checked out a dozen more books from the library on punctuation, sentence mechanics, and more. Ien wanted the document to be so much like a novel that he even gave it a title that you suggested. He would have given it chapters, but I told him it wasn't that serious. Without you, Dyrain, I honestly believe my boy would be more focused on video games than trying to learn where to put a question mark. Ien is even having second thoughts on wanting to one day become an astronaut and is considering becoming a writer instead. I do understand the questions you ask my son because those are some of the same ones we ask each other when we read from the notebook or when the older aliens gave us a rundown of our history. We are confused almost as much as you. Think of it this way: people who believe in God don't necessarily agree with or interpret the Bible the exact same way because some things in the Bible may be confusing or hard for humans to believe. With that being said, that doesn't mean there isn't a God or that the Bible isn't true. I first read the Bible ten years ago and still do to this day. I find things in it that make me wonder how it can be real. Maybe God wanted the Bible to be full of confusion or maybe the ones who don't understand it are just ignorant. Regardless of the confusion, I still believe in your God and that means a whole lot coming from an alien. I see God's proof of existence around us every day. My son and I are looking for some of that same proof for our existence. That question you asked about controlling the weather and the future is one that I will surely ask if I ever see AWE. The only way we will get answers is after your document is fulfilled. Yes, it will be over thirty years from now, but that's all the hope my son and I have to hold on to. We are living for that moment. I want to know what we really looked like, I want to know where we're from, I want to know why we don't sleep and how Vrokma found us. Those are some of the many questions

I can't wait to one day find out. I want to know everything there is about who we are.

Your help is extraordinary to us in a precious way. You're more than just a pen pal. I don't want you to stop being my son's friend. If it is beginning to take a toll on you, I urge you to take a break until you think you have enough energy or time for us. I beg you not to stop your contact with us. I would even understand if you stayed out of contact with us for several months, but please don't stop being our friend.

Sincerely, Cortez Green

Saturday, June 14, couldn't have arrived quickly enough for the girls. After having one of the roughest weeks of their lives, they couldn't wait to finally do something fun. No more dealing with crazy neighbors or tomato gardens. No more staying inside on sunny days. The girls' punishment was in the history books, and the big day had finally come. They took turns helping one another do up their hair in the signature SkijFris double ponytail.

"Imagine if Mom would have let us dye our hair blue," Olina said to Kamora's reflection in the mirror.

"I know, right? We would have been rocking hot," Kamora said as she finished with Olina's hair. "But at least SkijFris will see our double ponytails."

The girls gleefully took off outside, all ready to go.

Mrs. Popsic smiled to herself when she noticed the girls were missing from their room, as she knew there was a good chance they were already in the van. "Are you ready, Sholt?" she asked her husband.

"Yes, honey," Mr. Popsic answered while he tied his shoe, but his answer was drowned out by the van's obnoxious horn. Mr. Popsic winced as the horn made the headache he had worse, but he tried not to get angry, as he knew the girls were just beyond excited.

A couple of minutes later, Mr. and Mrs. Popsic joked with each other as they headed to the van.

"I wonder why they're in such a rush," Mrs. Popsic joked.

"Maybe it has something to do with that Frisbee girl," Mr. Popsic said, rolling his eyes.

"Don't let them hear you get their favorite celebrity's name wrong," Mrs. Popsic teased. She got into in the van after her husband opened the door for her.

Kamora and Olina were chatting with Sammy on the BB.

"The weight program Coach Ellis has us on is way harder than what I did in high school. It's been a week and a half, and I've already gained about five pounds, no lie," Sammy said to his sisters.

"I like your new haircut," Kamora told her brother before passing the BB around for her parents to see.

Mrs. Popsic frowned after seeing the hairstyle on Sammy. "What do you think, Sholt?" she asked.

Mr. Popsic glanced at Sammy on the BB while trying to drive at the same time. "Yeah, uh …" he began but didn't finish.

"You didn't even look at it, Sholt," she said before facing Sammy again. "I think you need to grow all your hair back. That mohawk doesn't look charming at all," she huffed, passing the BB back to Kamora.

Olina grabbed the BB from Kamora. "When we see SkijFris, I'll tell her to also give you a thumb. I'll let you see her too, but you have to make sure you're on your BB to see her or else you'll miss her because the satellite for the eqi is banned from the mall," Olina excitedly explained.

"I'll probably be napping when you guys get to the mall," Sammy said, smiling.

The BB shut off a couple of seconds after Sammy spoke. Olina thought the BB shut down because the battery was low. "I thought you charged the stupid battery, Kamora. I was going to ask Sammy if I can keep some of my toys in his room until he comes back," Olina said.

Kamora grabbed her BB from Olina's lap and pulled out the battery. It had a full charge, so she looked for another problem. She nearly dropped it when her dad suddenly shouted.

"Good grief!" Mr. Popsic yelled and angrily hit the steering wheel with his hand as the van slowed to a stop. He had struck the steering wheel harder than he thought. "Ouch!" he yelped in pain. Hitting the steering wheel sent a vibration from his hands all the way up to his head, adding more pressure to his headache. Mr. Popsic seemed to know before everyone else why everything in the van began shutting down.

"Pull over, Mr. Popsic," an officer's voice said from the police com. The van fully shut down after Mr. Popsic pulled to the side of the road. Mrs. Popsic was upset at her husband for getting pulled over.

"Why were you speeding, Sholt? You know the spedensors in the street go off when you're driving too fast." Mrs. Popsic shook her head in disgust.

"I wasn't even going that fast. Could you get me some medicine for my head, darling?" Mr. Popsic looked pink in the face.

Mrs. Popsic aggressively searched through her purse.

The girls looked around in confusion. "You're going to make us late, Dad. We have to get to the mall before anybody else so we can be the first ones in line," Olina whined desperately.

Kamora sat silently, nodding in agreement with her sister.

Mrs. Popsic passed her husband a medicine tablet, but he accidently dropped it out of frustration. Mr. Popsic looked on the van floor and between the seats for the tablet. Knowing the girls were mad at him for getting pulled over, he didn't bother to ask them for help in his search.

"Here, Sholt." Mrs. Popsic gave him another pill.

Mr. Popsic quickly swallowed the pill with his wife's bottle of water, which he roughly grabbed from her hand.

"Don't snatch it from me," Mrs. Popsic said, irritated.

"I didn't snatch it, and if I did, I'm sorry. You don't have to be mad at me, Dyrain," Mr. Popsic said.

"How can I not be when you were ticketed three times in almost a year for speeding?" Mrs. Popsic threw her arms up toward the ceiling of the van.

Mr. Popsic rubbed his sweaty hands through his hair to dry them. He was beyond frustrated that he was about to have an extra bill added on to his old ticket bills he hadn't paid yet. His head throbbed like a heartbeat, thinking about how the girls would stay mad at him for making them late to the mall, and the more he saw his wife staring at him from his peripheral view, the more his palms continued to sweat. Mr. Popsic silently looked forward, waiting for the police officer to let him go. A minute went by without a word from the police com. Mr. Popsic refused to let another minute go by in silence. In an attempt to gain some sympathy, he complained to his family about how much his head was hurting before he was pulled over and mentioned that the medicine he just took was making him feel better.

"I didn't know there was headache medicine out there that worked in seconds," Kamora said sarcastically.

"Are you trying to hint that the reason you were pulled over is because your head is—or was—hurting?" Mrs. Popsic's cheeks rested heavily on her jaw.

Mr. Popsic ignored her question. He wasn't happy with the response he got with the first excuse he used, so he tried sneaking in another excuse. "I never would have been stopped if I didn't care about getting the girls to the mall on time," Mr. Popsic said. Seeing the unmoved looks on Kamora's and Olina's faces in the rearview mirror, he then moved on to plan C. "If you guys really look at the big picture …"—Mr. Popsic hesitated thoughtfully—"not a single person agrees with this new spedensor thing. I like the old system better. We all do. It's not fair how a thing built in concrete can clock a person's speed and trigger it off for police officers who sit their lazy butts in an office miles away to write somebody a ticket. You would think with this new 'efficient' system that a person could at least keep driving while the ticket is being docked, clocked, or whatever. Hurt us two ways, why dontcha, despite the new technology. The cops should just go back to pulling people over themselves," Mr. Popsic preached, waiting for his wife to agree.

The officer spoke from the police com before Mrs. Popsic could disagree with her husband. "Are you done with your tirade, Mr. Popsic? I understand your frustration, sir, but please understand that the spedensor system gives us officers time to deal with more important issues on the streets. We love the new system," the police officer said.

Mr. Popsic repeated the officer's last sentence in a mocking whisper.

"Excuse me?" the officer barked.

Mr. Popsic made googly-eyed faces at the police com.

"Stop it, Sholt! You're acting childish!" Mrs. Popsic raised her voice, utterly appalled.

"It's not like the officer can see me," Mr. Popsic whispered, keeping the funny faces going.

The officer heard everything. "I know what you must be going through, Mrs. Popsic," the officer said. "Seems he has too much testosterone for that little body to hold. Well, I'm all done with the ticket process; you all can be on your way—and say hi to SkijFris for me, girls." The police com shut off.

Mr. Popsic couldn't believe what the officer had just said about him. *What … ha … was she … she just called me … she really said that about me?* Mr. Popsic's mind blew a gasket. It took him close to five seconds to snap out of his deer-in-headlights look before he went ballistic on the police com, trying his best to break it.

Mrs. Popsic grabbed her husband's arms, forcing him to stop his attack on the police com. "What's gotten into you, Sholt?" Mrs. Popsic placed her husband's hands on the steering wheel.

Mr. Popsic took his hands off the steering wheel and folded his arms. Kamora screamed for her dad to drive. He refused, keeping his arms folded. Olina became so upset that she began to cry.

"Mom, tell Dad to drive!" Kamora yelled.

Mr. Popsic didn't budge to the cries and screams roaring from the back of the van.

Mrs. Popsic told him he was sleeping in the front room tonight, yet she got no reaction. She angrily opened her door and jumped out to walk to the driver's side of the van. She yanked Mr. Popsic's door open and used her heavy arm to shove him out of the driver's seat and over to the passenger seat. Olina's cries simmered down a bit once she saw her mom take the wheel.

"If I knew how to drive, I would have done just what you did, Mom." Kamora smiled.

Mrs. Popsic and the girls ignored Mr. Popsic for the rest of the drive as he pouted and mumbled to himself. "She really doesn't know how tall I am. Just because it shows a height of five foot five on my license doesn't mean I haven't grown since then. Officer of the law, my foot. What police officer conducts herself in that manner? I think I'm going to file a complaint." Mr. Popsic finished pouting.

They arrived at the NewPark Mall in Newark seven minutes behind their intended time.

Olina frowned when she saw the mall parking lot full of cars. "He made us late!" Olina cried out.

Three security guards stood by the entrance, directing cars to the lot. "It's going to be fifteen dollars for parking," one of the security guards told Mrs. Popsic. Kamora excitedly dug through her mom's purse and gave her the money before they were allowed to enter.

"All my years I've been coming here, this lot has never been so full of cars. Oh my," Mrs. Popsic said as she circled the parking lot until she was able to park. "Hold on, girls. Let me put the car in park before you get out. Are you still pouting, Sholt?" she asked.

Mr. Popsic looked away from his wife with his arms folded and bottom lip tucked between his teeth.

"Fine. You stay in the van." Mrs. Popsic closed the van door.

Kamora and Olina hadn't realized they had left their mom behind. The two had already made it into the mall as their mom was just shutting the door to the van. Mrs. Popsic called Olina on her Chit Chat.

"Hello," Kamora answered.

"You guys left me. Wait by the doors until I come in," Mrs. Popsic told Kamora.

"We can't, Mom. If we do, Olina and I will lose our spot in line," Kamora said excitedly.

Mrs. Popsic hung the phone up seconds later after she walked into the mall. It was total chaos inside. She saw woi everywhere with their cameras. Thousands of SkijFris fans filled the shopping center. Almost all the fans wore SkijFris-brand clothing. Mrs. Popsic looked up to the second floor to see security aggressively forcing the crowd of teenagers back from the balcony after it started shaking. Mrs. Popsic was having a hard time finding her daughters until she finally spotted Olina's wheelchair.

"Over here, Mom!" Olina waved her arm in the air.

Mrs. Popsic joined her daughters in the long line. "Thank God you're on the first floor. Don't go running off like that without me next time," Mrs. Popsic said.

Kamora looked around with amazement, but Olina was jealous and frustrated by what she saw. "Look at all the girls with the scotch-blue hair! That boy up there has scotch-blue hair also! Look, Kamora!" Olina pointed. "I wish Mother would have let us dye our hair scotch blue," Olina said as though her mom weren't present.

"Your double ponytail looks good." Mrs. Popsic fluffed it up for Olina. She looked around at the sea of teenagers again. She couldn't believe all the people that packed the mall on this Saturday afternoon, especially after seeing SkijFris's picture for the first time on posters that decorated the entire mall. "Tell me again, what is she famous for? I don't want to sound like the critical parent, but I can't see why people are flocking to see her. She looks funny, and I can't believe they would put her face on the same wall with the letters that celebrated the hundred-year anniversary of the national anthem a few months ago." Mrs. Popsic grimaced. "The last time I saw so many people in a mall was when I was a teenager, and it still wasn't this many people in line waiting to see that, um, what's his name? That guy—the tall guy from the Utah Jazz." Mrs. Popsic tried remembering the name.

The girls couldn't care less what their mom was saying. They became excited with the sudden eruption of screams that came from the kids close to the front of the line. Olina forgot she was in a wheelchair for a moment. Her chair bumped hard into a kid's leg when she pushed forward in excitement. The boy fell to the floor, but quickly jumped back to his feet.

"I'm sorry," Olina said, feeling bad.

The boy didn't seem to care that she'd run into him. He turned around to Olina with a smile on his face and said, "I think it's her! I think SkijFris just walked in!"

Olina craned her neck to look toward the front, but it seemed the farther she looked down the line, the taller people became. Olina couldn't see anything but the backs of the fans who were also trying to scope out SkijFris. Olina quickly turned her attention to Kamora, who was also desperately trying to catch a glimpse of the reality star. "Do you see her, Kamora?" Olina excitedly asked.

Kamora moved side to side and bounced up and down like everyone else in front of her. Mrs. Popsic found herself following the movement of the crowd until she noticed Olina having the hardest time of all getting a good view. Sadness flowed through Mrs. Popsic's body as she watched her daughter. A slow, deep breath and a dry swallow didn't make her feel better. This was another one of those times when she felt bad for Olina being in a wheelchair. Mrs. Popsic didn't know what to do to help her daughter, and she felt helpless just like Olina was feeling at that moment. Mrs. Popsic desperately looked around the mall to see if she could see other handicapped children. She quickly spotted a few upstairs on the second floor, and after looking for a couple of more minutes, she noticed a dozen or so other handicapped children, just like Olina, on the first floor. This settled Mrs. Popsic's emotions down. It made her feel a lot better that she and Olina weren't alone in that regard.

The screams from the fans became louder.

"Can you see her, Mom?" Olina asked her mother after being ignored by Kamora.

"No, honey. It's very hard for me to see anything with all these people in front of me," Mrs. Popsic said, trying to make her daughter feel better.

Just then, the fans from the first floor turned their screams to the crowd on the second floor. The same little boy Olina had knocked down was pointing up toward the second floor. "Look! The balcony is about to fall!" he screamed in fright.

The people below watched helplessly in horror. Everything seemed to move in slow motion. Some of the people on the first floor slowly backed away toward the doors, but the majority just stood there staring, unsure of what to do. The loud snap of the balcony coming apart sounded like two cars colliding. Like other parents in the crowd, Mrs. Popsic pulled her daughters toward her and wrapped her arms around them, shielding them from the terror coming their way. The fans' screams of excitement quickly turned to screams of fright as they watched people begin to fall from the balcony.

Out of seemingly nowhere, a red burst of light darted over the crowd of people on the first floor and caught the first person to fall, which turned out to be a twelve-year-old girl. The savior quickly and softly planted the girl on her feet. It took only a few seconds for the flash of light to save the rest of the people falling to their potential deaths. The light then flew up to the second floor and welded the metal balcony back together with the zoom of a red laser. Satisfied that the balcony was strong enough to hold the people again, the flash retrieved all the people who fell from the second floor and placed them back to their original spots.

"It's Superman!" the young boy Olina knocked to the ground earlier yelled out.

"It can't be Superman because she's a woman," another kid said.

"It's Superwoman," a parent uttered in amazement.

The flash was now at a standstill and the people could get a good look at what or who it was.

"It's SkijFris," Olina said in a low, surprised voice.

The rest of the fans were still trying to understand what had just happened. The shocked crowd had mixed feelings. Some people were cheering, some were crying, and others were shouting incoherently.

SkijFris floated in the air with her hands on her hips.

Her right knee was up in a karate-kick position. SkijFris slowly looked up, down, and all around herself to see what in the world was holding her up. She didn't see anything. She stretched her eyes wide in an attempt to wake herself up in case this was all a dream. She wanted to smack herself or find some water to toss on her face, but she didn't want the crowd to see she was just as surprised as they were that she was a flying superhero. So many thoughts raced through the reality star's head at that moment. *Maybe this is some kind of out-of-body experience*, she thought. SkijFris felt shivers of excitement going all throughout her body. She couldn't believe or understand how all this was happening. *My dream of becoming Superman is really happening, and it's not a dream*, SkijFris thought while still floating in the air.

She was pulled away from her thoughts by an angry voice. "What is this, a game to you people? You don't put people's lives in jeopardy for media attention or for any kind of entertainment. When I get done suing you and every person that had something to do with putting me and my family's life in danger, your career will be finished!" a parent aggressively yelled at SkijFris before storming out of the mall with her four kids. Other parents agreed and starting shouting at her as well.

SkijFris didn't expect the angry response from the people. She thought everybody would be praising her for somehow saving these lives. "No, no, wait … I di … no, I didn't have anything to do with what happened," SkijFris stuttered. She realized she had to tell the truth to her fans so they wouldn't all leave the mall. "Please believe me. I'm just as surprised as you at what just happen—"

"Oh yeah. You just magically gained the ability to fly. Stop the nonsense. You planned for everything to go down the way it went. You could have at least put safety mats or nets on the floor just in case somebody did hit the floor," another parent scolded SkijFris.

The security and the woi also looked confused by what had just happened. "This publicity stunt has to be the best one SkijFris has ever done!" a woi member shouted.

Most fans began to walk toward the exit. SkijFris became desperate. She wanted to prove that she didn't have anything to do with what happened. "Please don't go. Let me explain myself to you. You're my fans, I love you, and I wouldn't do anything to put your lives in jeopardy." She flew toward the exit to block off the rest of the people. She slowly turned herself all the way around, showing the crowd she didn't have anything attached to her to make her fly. She kicked off her shoes and held them in the air toward the people to prove they weren't Vultures. The fans stood there looking and listening for about a half a minute, until someone finally spoke out.

"We don't care if you're not wearing Vultures or don't have a Sky Pack on! We have had enough of your stunts for today, so move out of our way," a man standing a few feet from SkijFris yelled.

"Yeah, get outta the way." The young boy Olina knocked to the ground earlier stuck his tongue out at SkijFris.

SkijFris, desperate and not knowing what to say, instinctively grabbed the man's wrist to hold him back from going out the door.

"Are you crazy, lady?" he asked as he jerked his arm from her grasp. "Now you'll be charged with assault and kidnapping for holding me against my will!"

All SkijFris could think of was how unfairly she was being treated by fans she thought were loyal to her. "What do I have to do to make you guys believe me?" She pleaded, sad, frustrated, and enraged at the same time. She couldn't think of any way to convince the crowd to listen to her. SkijFris was now angry enough to test her power in a way her fans wouldn't like. She knew there'd be no going back once she decided to use her newfound power in a forceful way. Experiencing a mixture of emotions having been pushed to this point and being curious to know the limits of the power she possessed, she was ready to live out what she had always dreamed about as a kid. One of her many Superman memories as a youngster flew through her mind before she explored her powers:

> *(July 24, 2011) "Janet, how many times do I have to tell you that you're not a boy and that an eight-year-old girl shouldn't be fighting with boys?" Janet's dad wiped the blood off her elbow.*
>
> *"They started it, Dad. They took the Superman cape I got for my birthday. They said I couldn't be Superman because I was a girl. That made me mad."*
>
> *"I will go get your cape back or buy you another one, but you promise me you won't fight anymore," her father demanded.*
>
> *"If I could fight like Superman, I could fly them to the sky, and their mommies and daddies could never see them again, right, Daddy?"*
>
> *"Yeah, I guess so. Promise me you will try to keep your hands to yourself, and not only will I buy you a new cape, but we can go around the corner for some ice cream," he put a Band-Aid on his daughter's elbow.*
>
> *"Oh, I promise, I promise," the child assured as she hugged her daddy.*

SkijFris smiled sneakily at the man who'd threatened her. "Actually, *this* would more likely be considered an assault," she said as she grabbed him by his ankle and flung him to the other side of the mall, which was over a thousand feet long. He sailed screaming around several corners to finally end up in a store called Sleep Zone, where he slammed into a bed and uncomfortably passed out. SkijFris was again surprised by her power and how easy the man was to pick up and throw.

"Unbelievable." Kamora's eyes followed the man until he was out of view.

"No, kid, it's believable," SkijFris replied.

Kamora, who stood about thirty feet away with her back to SkijFris, wondered how was it possible for SkijFris to not only toss the man like a feather but also hear what she had said.

A security guard came running up to SkijFris. "I understand you're upset, but if you continue to block the exit, you will be run over by the crowd in the stampede that's about to take place."

"You must have missed what I just did to the last guy." SkijFris placed one finger under the guard's chiseled chin. "Here, I'll show you," she said.

The six-foot-four security guard smiled off her threat. "I'm just trying to do my job, lady. I'm not trying to be part of your stunt, so please just move before I move you myself."

It took just one finger to toss the guard up over a hundred feet to the ceiling of the mall. Luckily, he was able to hold on to one of the poles that held a large poster of SkijFris's face. He was now scared for his life as he held on tightly.

"Look what all those days in the gym prepared you for. Hope you can hold on," SkijFris said, laughing and pointing up at the security guard. Thirteen other security guards joined the first guard on the pole after they tried apprehending SkijFris.

"I don't know what's going on here, but I know I don't get paid enough for this," the last remaining security guard said as he ran for the side emergency exit.

But in true Superman style, SkijFris ripped the *S* from her name on her shirt and threw it at the guard before he could make an escape. "Gotcha!" SkijFris shouted triumphantly as she watched the *S* wrap around the security guard.

Her fans were now to the point where they were ready to take justice into their own hands.

"We have had enough of you, young lady!" an older man banged his cane against the floor.

That got the crowd of people going. They began to rush toward the exit where SkijFris stood.

SkijFris panicked in excitement, not fear, as she had so many choices of weapons, but didn't know which one to unleash on her fans turned enemies. She mimicked the 1980 *Superman II* movie scene when General Zod and two of his soldiers stopped a hostile crowd coming toward them. She put her hands behind her and placed her legs about seven inches apart while drawing in a deep breath, and then she quickly exhaled the air toward the people. The air burst from her mouth like a sharp, strong wind, pushing everyone back. SkijFris didn't care about the senior citizens, the handicapped, or even the babies that were being hit with the force of her wrath. People were being blown in every direction. SkijFris continued to blast the crowd for a good three minutes. Most of the fans who weren't smart enough to back down were rendered unconscious.

"Why are you doing this?" an angry teenager wailed as she held her unconscious friend in her arms.

SkijFris ignored her, fully in AWE of the strength of her own power. She was convinced that this new power was indeed the real thing and that nobody else had it but her, because if they did, they would have taken advantage of it like she was about to do. SkijFris was ready to take over the world.

Police officers called to the scene ten minutes earlier then arrived in full force. The thirty-three officers rushed into the mall with their weapons drawn.

"Looks like a hurricane hit this place," an officer said as he looked around in disbelief.

One of the officers recognized the reality star when entering the building. "Are you okay, SkijFris? Where are the terrorists?" The officer asked with his gun drawn.

"They told you guys terrorists did this? How dare they give somebody credit for my mess." SkijFris laughed. She didn't waste any time shooting heat lasers from her eyes at each officer's gun. The heat from the lasers instantly made every single officer drop his or her weapon.

"How did you do that?" an officer cried, his hands singed.

The officers scrambled for their guns but couldn't pick them up off the ground.

"Too hot to handle, huh? I'll show you that hurricane you wanted to see," SkijFris said as she flew up and around the police, showing off her power. "And this is without the Vultures or Sky Pack!" she bragged.

The police officers looked up at SkijFris as she flew around. "This must be *Con Trick U Liar,*" an officer blurted out.

"Yeah, and I bet the chief had something to do with this," another officer said, chuckling.

If the other officers believed they were a part of the *Con Trick U Liar* show, they soon changed that thought after SkijFris flew back down toward them like a rocket, knocking every single one of them through the windows back outside.

SkijFris floated in the air with her chest pumped out proudly. She suddenly realized she had developed the signature Superman curly string of hair, though hers hung from her forehead all the way to her stomach. She had a great time watching everyone suffer in confusion.

"I'm just getting started with you people," SkijFris said as she landed on the ground. She thought of all the powers Superman had so that she could use them all on her prior fans while making her rounds. The tossing, kicking, blowing people back and forth went on until a security guard fell to his death. That got everyone's attention, including SkijFris's. SkijFris flew toward the guard. She tried bringing him back to life by blowing air in his lungs and pumping his chest.

"You're blowing too hard," a girl said.

"Don't push his chest that hard!" a different girl yelled.

"Don't have the power to bring him back to life, huh? You can kill that poor man, but you can't give him life? What a shame," a woman angrily mocked SkijFris's powers.

SkijFris jumped up in anger. "I can't win for nothing. Earlier I tried telling you people I had nothing to do with the collapse of the balcony, and then I tried begging you guys to listen to me and not to leave the mall, and now I try to save this man's life, but you scold me. Half of you parents in here didn't even want to pay the full price for your kids to meet me even after I gave you half price off. You're selfish. All of you." SkijFris's hair turned purple.

"We don't care if you get mad," a lady said with authority.

Her comment sent SkijFris even further over the top. SkijFris showed no mercy and blew freezing air forcefully out of her nostrils at the lady until the lady was frozen in ice. The woman's two daughters cried and frantically banged the ice that covered their mother, but to no avail.

"Superman never even did that one," SkijFris boasted. She moved on to the next person without remorse. She flew all the way up to the ceiling of the mall and back down on top of a man's head, knocking him below the foundation of the mall. The crowd erupted into chaos with every still-conscious person running into each other, trying to get away as SkijFris took her power to the next level.

SkijFris made her next move toward a boy on crutches. "When was the last time you were able to walk on your own?" she asked him, pretending like she cared.

Olina wasn't very far from the boy and couldn't keep silent. "No, don't hurt him, SkijFris!"

SkijFris turned to Olina and laughed. "Don't worry. I'll ask you the same question next." SkijFris turned back to the boy on crutches. A plastic cup suddenly struck the back of her head, taking her attention away from the boy for the second time.

Sholt hoped his throw was enough of a distraction to help Olina get past the reality star gone bad. "Come on, honey! Hurry! Hurry!" Sholt screamed.

That second distraction gave the boy enough time to get lost in the crowd.

"Look what you did. You helped the cripple get away. Now I'll hurt your daughter instead." SkijFris knelt on one knee as she braced herself to take off straight into Olina.

Sholt could only watch in horror. He couldn't make a move or a sound. His body was paralyzed from fear of what was going to happen to his precious Olina.

At that moment, Olina lost all the love she ever had for SkijFris. And with that loss of love, the power in SkijFris was no more. Olina quickly covered her face in fear, but not before she screamed, "I hate you, SkijFris!" SkijFris flew up into the air, but quickly fell back down flat on her belly, knocking the wind from her lungs.

Slowly but surely, Sholt came out of his daze. He stomped on SkijFris unintentionally to grab Olina's chair and push her to safety.

"'Snap back to reality. Oh, there goes gravity,'" Sholt

mocked SkijFris's quick downfall as he ran out of the mall with his family.

Later on that night back at 318674 Glencoe Drive, the Popsics talked about the hot topic. Sammy joined in on the talk from his BB.

"Dad saving me from SkijFris wasn't even the best part. It was when he started to rap." Olina rolled her wheelchair back and forth, giggling.

"Dad? Rapping? I don't believe it. What do you know about rap, Dad?" Sammy chuckled.

"First of all"—Sholt fixed his glasses with one finger as he explained himself—"I was rapping me some Eminem, someone you young people wouldn't know about today. That's when rap used to be fun, unlike the nonsense rap of today."

"I know who he is, and for your information, Dad, everybody calls him Em," Kamora said.

"He still raps?" Sholt looked surprised.

"No, he's like a hundred years old," Kamora said sarcastically.

"Doesn't he have a grandson who raps?" Mrs. Popsic blurted out. Her question went unanswered due to the ten o'clock news coming on. The family didn't want to miss this.

"This is Naras Calit for *On the Spot News*. Will Iran be protected under the new NATO policy for their weapon sanction violation? Do Americans think the new age limit of thirty-two to be president of the United States is a way to make other countries think we're smarter than we really are after we failed to get the number-one place for the ECC Test? But before those two topics, we will talk about everybody's favorite reality star, SkijFris, who got her start on *Local Celebrity*. SkijFris rose through the pop culture scene in popularity surpassing all her other reality counterparts, but today, she rose in a much different way. It was something like a scene from last year's blockbuster DC Comics second-installment movie *Flash: School of the Gladiators*. Onlookers may as well have been watching Flash take on the twin villain brothers, Lazor and Gosp, in the famous shopping mall scene. An event like nothing ever before seen or heard of—unless it involved magicians at a circus or actors in a movie—took place today at NewPark Mall in Newark, California. Entertainment and mystery have always played a big role in American culture since way before Harry Houdini or Charlie Chaplin graced the big stage. Today may have changed the way America—the world—will look at entertainment from now on, thanks to the reality of this reality star. Most of tonight's news will reflect on the rise and fall— and I mean literally a fall—of a reality icon that in the eyes of many was so famous that she could have been president of any country in the world if she wanted to."

After watching the news for twenty-three minutes, the family was stunned to hear that SkijFris acted alone, without any assistance from her family, friends, employees, the mall managers—everyone denied participating in what everyone had thought was a publicity stunt gone bad.

"How could she fly and do all that stuff without help? How can you guys say she didn't even have the Vultures or Sky Pack? None of what SkijFris supposedly did by herself makes sense unless she has supernatural powers, and we know that's not the case," Kamora lectured the TV.

"I still can't get over her blowing ice out of her mouth." Mr. Popsic looked confused.

Olina just shook her head sadly after the news was over.

Kamora hugged her sister to make her feel better. "Don't worry, Olina. You will get over it." Kamora smiled.

Olina hugged her sister back and left the front room to head for bed.

"Yeah, I'm right behind you, sis. Good night, Mother and Father." Kamora followed her sister.

"Good night, my darlings. I'm kind of sleepy myself." Mrs. Popsic struggled to get off the sofa before heading to bed.

Mr. Popsic sat alone in the front room. "Finally, the coast is clear," Mr. Popsic mumbled to himself as he began to check his scratch-off ticket.

Olina caught her dad off guard, coming back into the living room. Olina fell into her dad's arms, giving him a big hug. "I forgot to thank you for being there for me," Olina softly said.

"That's what dads are for." Mr. Popsic smiled. "I promise you will never go through something like that again. I don't think *anybody* will go through something that crazy again. The only good thing about what happened is that I think I finally lost my headache in all the excitement. Tomorrow will bring a better day." Mr. Popsic chuckled and kissed his youngest daughter on the forehead without realizing his Goldruption ticket had fallen from underneath his leg.

"Oooh! Dad, you promised Mom you wouldn't buy any more tickets, and this is one of those fifty-dollar ones." Olina held it in her hand.

Mr. Popsic laughed nervously and hurriedly snatched the ticket back from his daughter, telling her good night before slipping into his bedroom.

Dyrain's Dictionary

1) Antwaun Collier is a former Oklahoma Sooner basketball player.

2) *BB* stands for *Book Blog*. The BB is a Microsoft edition that lets the consumer stay up to date with the celebrity lifestyle. The device is designed in the form of a book and gives the BB owner access to the stars' day-to-day lives, from what they buy at the store to the kind of gas they put in their vehicles to who they talked on the phone with and so on.

3) Blazet is like a microwave, but it allows things such as aluminum and metal to be heated up along with the food.

4) Blue Ivy is a theater actress.

5) Bodtic is an elevator without the up-and-down movement used in the search of a person's body and their belongings during airport security checks.

6) *Cerminize* is a word from the movie *Half a Howl* used in the chanting for the birthright of a crown.

7) CloutCrowd is a celebrity social networking site operated by fans that help in facilitating stars' careers.

8) Codar is used for the operation of the VM.

9) Contact shades are gel-coated films worn on the eyelashes for constant cleansing of the contact lenses.

10) *Con Trick U Liar* is TV show where known pranksters are the ones being pranked.

11) Corey Randolph is a former Oklahoma Sooner basketball player.

12) Chit Chat is a cell phone that automatically reads the lips of the talker while transferring the words to the listener's phone, where it can be seen or heard. The Chit Chat is also known as the "public private phone" because it allows a person to whisper while in a loud environment and still be heard by the listener in the caller's regular voice.

13) Doggyshire is a doghouse equipped with cleaning necessities to clean both the doghouse and the dog.

14) *ECC* stands for *Every Country Counts*. It's when countries participate in a smart test once a year that's based on a mixture of common sense and school smarts.

15) *ENBA* stands for *Europe National Basketball Association*. It's an extension of the NBA overseas, and I assume you know what the NBA is.

16) Eqi is a foldable laptop device that can be folded so small that it can fit into a person's pocket. The eqi is used for the live streaming of a celebrity's normal day-to-day life. The main feature of the eqi is to watch live entertainment in an accessible approach that's almost equal to being present at the live performance itself.

17) Fitted flash is a form of a flashlight that is worn as gloves.

18) *Flash: School of the Gladiators* is a DC Comics film.

19) Folik is a small tool used in the assisting of conditioning a single hair follicle.

20) Goldruption is a lottery scratch-off ticket.

21) Hulka spray is a healing formula for any kind of wound to the body. It miraculously rejuvenates the tissue and skin back to its original structure in seconds.

22) Humatizer is a tube mounted on a wall that blows out disinfectant air to kill germs.

23) *Local Celebrity* is a reality TV show about the most popular people from various neighborhoods trying to be the next reality star.

24) Lora Ramirez is the vice president of the United States.

25) Mahort clip is a stylish device used for emergency situations that is small enough to be attached to jewelry.

26) Noxturn chair is a wheelchair made for a heavyset person.

27) *On the Spot News* is a late-night news program about popular topics of that day.

28) Ose Peyha is a rapper.

29) PlayStation Infinito XR is based on a series of video games and live TV that runs concurrently.

30) Poj Rehabilitation Academy is a physical and educational training institution specifically for the children affected by the tainted debris from the 2012 space expedition.

31) Police com is a voice communication system located under the dashboards of vehicles for the police officer and the person or people in a civilian car to communicate with each other.

32) Rancea Sola is a pop singer from Europe who became a reality star in the United States.

33) Scholar chair is the most advanced wheelchair for the disabled.

34) Second coming speech is the speech for the return of a new wizpire.

35) SkijFris is a reality star.

36) Sky Pack is part of the Vulture brand. It's a wearable backpack with helium inside to help a person float in the air.

37) Sleep Zone is a bed store located in the NewPark Mall.
38) Smilt is a digital clamp-type comb used to get rid of all the uneven hair in one swoop.
39) Spedensors consist of metal sensors placed underground to help police officers with the ticketing of speeding drivers.
40) Teasec is an illegal camcorder in the form of a camouflage sticker that's used for spying on celebrities. People do this by mostly hiding the camcorder on light poles, fences, and trees near a celebrity's home.
41) *Thumb* is the slang word for *autograph*. This happens when a celebrity places a thumb on the autograph part of the BB to be sent to the fan.
42) Traveler's Circle is a delivery company that originated overseas with franchises all throughout the United States. The company is based on having members and consists of pickups instead of mailing. Let me be more specific with you, Dyrain. If you were a member of Traveler's Circle in Florida, but you had a taste for a pizza they sell in Texas, the only way you could get that pizza is to call a Traveler's Circle company in that Texas town to see when the next time a member from that town might be passing through Florida. Once it's verified that a member will be passing through, they will drop your pizza off at the closest Traveler's Circle for you to pick it up. I could give you more information, but I think you get the point.
43) Twitter is a social networking service that lets the fan and the celebrity communicate and follow each other mainly through texting.
44) Vitamin Q is the herbal supplement to help in the building process of paralyzed bones and damaged tissue.

45) VM is the ultimate upgrade of data storage of all sorts. New products being sold that contain data can also be transferred to the old VM.

46) Vultures are shoes that are operated by a computer to assist a person in levitating up to two hundred feet high. The Vultures are mostly used by circus performers.

47) William Hanson is a talk show host and author.

48) Wizpire is a half-wizard, half-vampire character from the movie *Half a Howl*.

49) Woi is SkijFris's personal camera crew she discovered from North Korea.

50) Zac Zookasmitchs is a high school basketball player.

51) Zoomeda is a machine being built for traveling purposes. Its goal is to get people from one place to another in less than five minutes, no matter how far away the destination is.

About the Author

Glynn Green was born and raised in Aurora, Illinois, and earned a bachelor's degree from Southern Illinois University in Carbondale. *My Pen Pal Ien* is his first book.

Printed in the United States
By Bookmasters